I0670942

Dick Prescott's First Year at West Point

Two Chums in the Cadet Gray

H. Irving Hancock

1st WORLD
LIBRARY
Literary Society

Dick Prescott's First Year at West Point

H. Irving Hancock

© 1st World Library – Literary Society, 2005
PO Box 2211
Fairfield, IA 52556
www.1stworldlibrary.org
First Edition

LCCN: 2006902701

Softcover ISBN: 1-4218-1833-7
Hardcover ISBN: 1-4218-1733-0
eBook ISBN: 1-4218-1933-3

Purchase *"Dick Prescott's First Year at West Point"*
as a traditional bound book at:
www.1stWorldLibrary.org/purchase.asp?ISBN=1-4218-1833-7

1st World Library Literary Society is a nonprofit
organization dedicated to promoting literacy by:

- Creating a free internet library accessible from any
  computer worldwide.
- Hosting writing competitions and offering book
  publishing scholarships.

**Readers interested in supporting literacy
through sponsorship, donations or
membership please contact:
literacy@1stworldlibrary.org
Check us out at: www.1stworldlibrary.ORG
and start downloading free ebooks today.**

Dick Prescott's First Year at West Point
contributed by Tim, Ed & Rodney
in support of
1st World Library Literary Society

CONTENTS

I.   "TWO TINY SPECKS OF NOTHING" ---------------------- 7

II.   THE TYRANNY OF THE CADET CORPORAL --------24

III.   THE "LUCKY" ONES TAKE UP THE NEW LIFE -----34

IV.   GREG'S CASE OF "BLUES" --------------------------------43

V.   CANDIDATE DODGE IS CRITICAL ----------------------50

VI.   IN THE HANDS OF THE YEARLING HAZERS ------58

VII.   A SUDDEN GRIND AT MATH---------------------------68

VIII.   DICK BONES TROUBLE ----------------------------------74

IX.   PLEBE PRESCOTT'S FIRST FIGHT ----------------------81

X.   THE "BEAST" WHO SCORED --------------------------88

XI.   HOW CADET DODGE HELD POST
        NUMBER THREE --94

XII.   PRESCOTT GETS NUMBER THREE------------------ 106

XIII.   THE SENTRY MAKES A CAPTURE-------------------- 116

XIV.   POOR GREG CAN'T EXPLAIN------------------------ 125

XV.   GREG OVERHEARS A PRETTY
        GIRL'S TRIBUTE-- 134

XVI.   TAPS SOUNDS ON SUMMER------------------------ 141

XVII.   MR. DODGE GOES CANVASSING------------------- 147

XVIII. THE PLEBE CLASS CHOOSES ITS
        PRESIDENT-- 152

XIX.   THE PROWLER IN QUARTERS ----------------------- 163

XX.   CONCLUSION --- 167

CHAPTER I

"TWO TINY SPECKS OF NOTHING"

"How do you feel, Dick! As spruce as you did an hour ago!"

Candidate Greg Holmes put the question with a half-nervous laugh. He spoke in a whisper, too, as if to keep his agitation from reaching the notice of any of the score or more of other young men in the room of Mr. Ward, the aged notary at West Point.

"I'll be glad when I see some daylight through the proceedings," Dick Prescott whispered in answer.

"I'm glad they allow us to talk here in undertones," pursued Greg.

"If we weren't allowed to do so, some of us would go suddenly crazy, utter a whoop and spring through one of the windows," grinned Dick.

For the tenth time he thrust his hands into his pockets - then as quickly drew them out again.

All of the young men now gathered in the room were candidates for cadetships at West Point; candidates who had been appointed by the Congressmen or Senators of their home districts or states, and who must now pass satisfactory physical and mental examinations, after which they would be enrolled as cadets in the United States Military Academy. Those of the cadets who thus passed the preliminary examinations, and who maintained good health and good standing in their classes during the following four years and three months would then be graduated from the Military Academy and forthwith be appointed second lieutenants in the Regular Army of the United States.

Hived in this room, awaiting their turn, a spirit of awe had gripped all these nervous young men.

Some of them dreaded a failure in the coming bodily tests before the keen-eyed, impartial surgeons of the United States Army.

Probably half of the boys in the room feared that they would fail in the academic examinations.

Boys? Some of the candidates didn't look the part. They had the physiques and general appearance, many of them, of men; for a candidate may be anywhere between the ages of seventeen and twenty-two years of age.

From all over the country they came. When the new, or plebe class should finally be assembled and put to work, that class would represent practically every state in the Union.

Readers of a former series of books, "THE HIGH SCHOOL BOYS SERIES," will not need to again be introduced to Dick Prescott and Greg Holmes. Such readers will well remember these two manly young Americans as members of that famous sextette, "Dick & Co.," famous in the annals of the good old Gridley High School.

Nor will such readers need to be told how Dick won, over the heads of forty competitors, the nomination of Congressman Spokes, the boy carrying all before him in a rigid competitive examination at the Gridley High School. The same readers will remember how Greg Holmes secured his own nomination from Senator Frayne. This was all related in the closing volume of the High School Series, "THE HIGH SCHOOL CAPTAIN OF THE TEAM."

Our former readers will also recall that Dave Darrin and Dan Daizell "ran away" with the nominations for cadetships at Annapolis, while Tom Reade and Harry Hazelton, the last of famous Dick & Co., went West seeking their careers as young engineers.

To be a cadet at West Point, and then to blossom out as an officer in the Regular Army - this had long been Dick's fondest hope. Greg, too, had caught the Army fever, and now suffered from it as severely as Dick Prescott himself.

And now, at what seemed like the critical moment, this tedious waiting was almost maddening.

Before Mr. Ward's desk stood a lonely looking young man, red faced and fidgeting as though he were going through a fearful ordeal.

"What on earth can they be doing to that fellow?" wondered Greg, in a barely audible undertone. "That fine-looking old gentleman can't be hazing a cadet?"

"No; but I wonder what the ordeal is," Dick whispered back. "I haven't seen a fellow look comfortable through it yet."

"Mr. Prescott!"

Dick started to his feet so suddenly that his right almost tripped over his left.

One of the other candidates near by tittered. That caused Dick's face to turn redder than ever.

Mr. Ward, however, looked up at the boy with a kindly smile.

"State your full name, Mr. Prescott."

Dick did so.

"When and where born? Give date and place."

By this time Dick was beginning to find his voice. The excess of color began to recede from his face. He had already, almost unconsciously, passed over the sealed envelope which he had received from the adjutant in a room on the same floor at headquarters.

Prescott was quickly breathing at his ease. He discovered that the entire ordeal consisted of giving his family history, with dates.

Then he stepped back. Another name was called.

"Don't let that rattle you a bit, Greg," whispered Dick, when he had dropped back into his seat beside his chum. "Mr. Ward doesn't do anything but take your pedigree."

"Mr. Holmes!"

Greg got up with nearly all of his self-possession about him. He was just returning to sit by his chum when the nattiest, sprucest-looking soldier imaginable, wearing the olive-drab fatigue uniform of the Army and overcoat to match, stepped into the room.

"The surgeons have directed me to bring down all the candidates who are through here," the orderly announced. "Follow me to the sidewalk, where you will fall in loosely, by twos, and follow me to the cadet hospital."

Among those of the candidates who had finished giving their pedigrees there was a rush that would put a spectator in mind almost of a football scrimmage. It represented merely the feverish anxiety of these young men to get through with the next stage in their awe-filled day.

"There are some marching down with us who won't be marching with us to the next place, I am afraid," whispered Holmes.

"I imagine so," whispered Dick, with a nod.

"Say," murmured Greg, his cheek suddenly blanching, "just how much chest expansion do the surgeons demand in the case of a fellow standing five-seven in his stocking feet?"

There was a note almost of panic in Greg's voice.

"Cheer up, Greg!" urged Dick, whose own lace was again flushing. "You've got chest expansion enough for a heavy-weight prize fighter."

"You must have the same, then. Is that so?" demanded Holmes. "What makes your face so red?"

"Just wondering," admitted Prescott, in a low voice, "whether I ever contracted any symptoms of football-player's heart."

"Bosh!" muttered Greg. "I never heard of any such disease."

"I never did either," Dick fidgeted. "But in the hour I've been at West Point I've concluded that people here know a heap of things that aren't even guessed at in the outside world."

"O-o-o-h! Say! Look!" murmured Greg in deep awe and admiring wonder. "They must be cadets!"

Eight young men in gray, marshaled by a section marcher, went swinging up the road with a marching rhythm so perfect that it was like music.

Each of these young men was clad in flawless gray, with black stripes and facings. Each young man wore his cadet fatigue cap at an exact angle. The long, caped gray overcoats looked as though they had been melted to the forms of their wearers.

No wonder Greg Holmes gave that involuntary gasp. He was having his first view of a small squad of real cadets.

Some of the candidates on the other sidewalk so far forgot themselves as to halt and all but stare at the natty young marching men opposite.

Then, all in an instant, the section marcher and his section had gone by.

"Don't anyone halt, please," cautioned the soldier orderly. "Keep your places in the line, young gentlemen, and keep moving right along."

So they reached the cadet hospital. The orderly marched them into a spacious, almost bare room on the ground floor and announced:

"I will report to the surgeon. Young gentlemen, wait until you are called."

"I wish I could carry myself and step the way that fellow does," whispered Dick, his admiring gaze following the retreating orderly.

"Well, that's what we've come here to learn," replied Greg. "That is, if we get by the doctors - and then the beastly academic grind."

Now, to keep his mind occupied, Dick Prescott fell to observing, covertly, the other candidates.

These were of all sorts and sizes. They represented all parts of the United States and every walk in social life. Out of the group were two or three who, judging by their clothing, might have been sons of washerwomen. There were other youngsters

H. Irving Hancock

whose general appearance and bearing seemed to proclaim that they came from homes of wealth. But the majority of the young men appeared to have come from the same walk in life as did Dick and Greg.

Our two young friends were by no means the most smartly nor the most correctly attired young men there. On their way to New York Prescott and Holmes had discovered, by taking mental notes of the other male passengers on the train, that these two Gridley boys had missed something from the most correct styles then prevailing in the larger cities.

Dick and Greg were both solidly and substantially attired, yet there was an indefinable something about them which proclaimed them to be young men from one of the smaller cities of the United States.

"I can see those medical big-wigs pawing me over now," shivered Greg. "I suppose, at a place as wonderful and as learned as West Point, the doctors are all fussy old men, with their gold-rimmed spectacles and shiny frock coats."

"Wait and see," advised Dick, trying to get a grip on himself to control his nervousness.

Another door opened, to admit a dandified and very smart-looking young officer, apparently about twenty-five years of age.

"You're all ready, young gentlemen?" he asked smilingly.

"We're waiting for the doctor," replied Greg, who was close to the door by which the officer had entered.

"I am one of the surgeons," replied the young officer pleasantly.

"Gee whiz!" remarked one raw-boned youth, in what was meant to be a confidential whisper, but which rose to a pitch that carried it around the room. "Say, he doesn't look much like our old saw-bones doc down home way!"

The surgeon was followed by a smart-looking soldier of the hospital corps, who started to close the shades of the room.

"You have all been to the treasurer's office and deposited your funds?" asked the young surgeon, turning again. This time his question appeared to be addressed to Dick more particularly than to anyone else.

"Why, no, sir," Prescott replied. "I have all my money in my pocket yet."

"Orderly!" spoke the surgeon to his own man of the hospital corps, who wheeled, brought his heels together and stood at attention. "Bring in that orderly who conducted the young gentlemen here."

"Yes, sir," replied the hospital orderly, wheeling about and vanishing from the room. He was back again in a moment with the soldier who had brought in this batch of candidates without interviewing the treasurer.

"Orderly," spoke the surgeon, "you have overlooked one part of your instructions. You did not take these candidates to the treasurer's office."

"No, sir."

"Do so now. Then conduct the candidates back here."

"Very good, sir."

Signing to the candidates to rise and follow him outside, the orderly himself led the way.

"Say, that was neatly done. No calling the man down; no bluster," whispered Greg as the candidates again walked along the sidewalk.

"It's the Army way, I take it," murmured Dick.

This time the orderly marched his awkward squad straight to the cadet store and into the treasurer's office.

"O-o-o-h!" groaned Greg in an undertone.

"What's the matter?" demanded Dick in a cautious whisper.

"This delay and killing suspense before we get before the doctors. I'll bet my fever has gone up above one hundred and three degrees!"

"Form in line, and each one of you turn in all his money," directed the treasurer crisply.

Each candidate was required to deposit with the treasurer the sum of one hundred dollars. In the event that the candidate "passed" successfully to enrollment in the cadet corps, then this money was to be applied to the purchase of things necessary for the new cadet to have. In case the candidate did not pass he would receive his hundred dollars back again - enough, in almost any case, to take the young man safely back to his home.

The first three men to step before the treasurer each turned in a few dollars in excess of the hundred.

Each was handed the treasurer's receipt for the exact amount that he deposited.

Then came a rather dazzlingly attired young man of at least twenty-one. He had watched the others and now, with an air of some importance, drew out a roll of considerable size. He detached two fifty-dollar bills and handed them to the treasurer, with the query:

"A century covers the deposit, doesn't it?"

Though the treasurer frowned slightly at the slang use of "century," he replied briskly:

"You must deposit all the money you have, Mr. Geroldstone."

"But that doesn't seem like a square deal," protested young Geroldstone. "I'll need some money for personal expenses, some for little dinners, something to spend on the young [Transcriber's note: word missing]"

"You'll need no money here, Mr. Geroldstone. Cadets are allowed no spending money outside of the so-called confectionery allowance, and that is charged to you from your pay."

"But I'm a big candy eater," urged Geroldstone, with a grin.

"No argument, if you please, sir!" rapped the treasurer rather sharply. "Turn over all your money and remember that you are on honor in the matter."

Mr. Geroldstone received a receipt for nine hundred and sixty-two dollars, plus a few small coins. As he turned away he muttered to one of his predecessors:

"Say, ain't that a good deal like a hold up?"

"Remember, young gentlemen, all the money you have," admonished the treasurer, as the line started to move again.

Thus commanded, the candidates went through all their pockets while standing awaiting their own turns.

Dick and Greg had so well calculated their traveling expenses that each turned in about twenty dollars above the required one hundred dollars.

This little transaction completed, the orderly turned and

marched them back at once to the hospital.

By this time some of the candidates had sufficiently overcome their nervousness to realize how raw and chilly this first day of March was. All of the candidates wore overcoats, though the outer garments worn by some of the young men, especially those who had journeyed hither from Southern States, were not of a weight to meet the March demands at hilly West Point, which lies exposed to the icy northern blasts down the Hudson River.

It looked as though it might snow at any moment. There was "ice in the air," as Greg Holmes expressed it.

So it was a welcome relief to all of the young candidates to find themselves once more inside the hospital building.

They were taken into the same room. During their absence the hospital corps orderly had distributed blankets, one on each chair.

"Each of you will please strip now," announced the same young medical officer, coming briskly into the room. "Strip as quickly as you can. Each man take a blanket and wrap it around himself while waiting."

Some of the young men looked startled, but all obeyed. In this stripping, and in the varied degrees of orderliness with which the different stacks of discarded clothing were piled it was rather easy to pick out the young men who had previously undressed in the dressing quarters of schools or colleges where athletics are a big feature.

"If we had a few tom-tom players we'd be ready with a fine imitation of an Indian war dance," muttered one of the candidates, gazing about him at his blanketed companions. There was a laugh, of course. These highly nervous youngsters were ready to laugh at anything just now.

"Is Mr. Geroldstone ready?" asked the hospital orderly, marching into the room.

"I will be, in five minutes or so," replied Geroldstone, slowly pulling his shirt off over his head.

"Mr. Danvers, then," called the orderly, consulting a slip of paper in his right hand.

Candidate Frank Danvers, a good-looking young man, self-contained, slight of build, not very tall, but very black as to hair, stepped forward.

"In here, sir," requested the hospital orderly, holding open the door. After Danvers had gone the other young men held their breath for a few moments - all except Geroldstone, who was still leisurely disrobing.

Back came Danvers after a few moments. Every candidate in the room looked at him inquiringly.

"Yes, gentlemen; I'm very happy to say that I passed," nodded Danvers, as he sprang across the room and began to don his clothes once more.

"Mr. Geroldstone!" called the orderly, and the big candidate went in.

An anxious twenty minutes passed - anxious alike for Geroldstone and for those who still dangled on tenterhooks in the outer room.

At last the candidate under fire came out, a sickly grin on his face. Though the others looked at him curiously, not a word did Geroldstone offer.

"The big fellow has failed; I'll bet," muttered Greg Holmes. "I'm sorry for him, poor fellow."

Still another candidate was now undergoing the ordeal inside. When he came out, nodding contentedly, the summons sounded:

"Mr. Prescott!"

"Brace up, Dick! You're all right," whispered Greg, with an affectionate pat on the shoulder as young Prescott rose, and, wrapping the blanket nervously around him, went through the doorway.

The same young medical officer, Lieutenant Herman, was in the other room. With him was an older medical officer, Captain Goodwin.

"Drop your blanket on that chair," nodded Lieutenant Herman. "Now, step over to the scales."

Dick's weight, stripped, was taken, as well as his height. These points Lieutenant Herman jotted down as Captain Goodwin called them off.

"Now, let me listen to your heart," directed the senior medical officer, picking up a stethoscope from his desk. The heart beat and sounds were examined from several points.

"Come here, Mr. Prescott," directed Captain Goodwin, opening another door and revealing a flight of stairs. "Run up these stairs and back, as fast as you can."

As Dick halted, after that feat, his heart action was again examined, this time by both surgeons. After that his lungs were examined. Then he was directed to lie on a table, while the areas over his other organs were thumped and listened to. Then the candidate was examined for deformities. He was ordered to march around the room, to run, to jump over a low stool, and perform other antics.

Then the two surgeons conferred briefly at the desk.

"You'll do, Mr. Prescott," announced Captain Goodwin.

"Thank you, sir," stammered Dick, the flush of happiness coming to his cheeks.

"You've taken part in school athletics, haven't you?" asked Lieutenant Herman.

"Yes, sir; captain of our football team last fall."

"You look it," nodded Lieutenant Herman pleasantly. "Take your blanket, Mr. Prescott. Orderly, call the next man."

As Dick strode back where he had left the others he heard the orderly call:

"Mr. Holmes."

"Go to it, old man. There's nothing to be afraid of," whispered Dick Prescott.

"They got through with you in mighty quick time," smiled one of the other candidates.

"Did they?" laughed Prescott. "It seemed to me as though the surgeons started yesterday and finished to-morrow."

Mr. Geroldstone had finished dressing and sat by, a sulky look on his face. He wanted to go back to cadet store, get his money and leave West Point instantly. But the orderly had told him he would have to wait until a report had been made out to the adjutant.

To Dick the minutes dragged until Greg Holmes appeared again. Truth to tell, Greg was much afraid that he had a slight trouble with his heart, and that this difficulty would hinder his passing. Dick, who was aware of his chum's dread, was anxious for Holmes. As soon as he had finished dressing he found himself pacing the floor.

It was quite a while ere Greg came out, but his quiet, happy smile told the story.

"Did they ask you questions about your heart?" asked Prescott in an undertone.

"Yes," admitted Greg, while he dropped his blanket and began hastily pulling on his clothes.

"You told the truth, didn't you?"

"Of course, I did," flushed Greg. "If I hadn't told the truth I wouldn't be fit to be an Army officer. But Captain Goodwin laughed at me."

"Then he didn't find anything much wrong with your heart!"

"He said he guessed I had had some discomfort at times, but that, if I would eat more slowly, and chew my food better, my stomach would get a rest and stop shoving my heart."

"Oh! Is that all that has been ailing you?" smiled Dick.

"According to Captain Goodwin it's enough. He says my trouble started only recently, and that I can be over the last sign of it in three days if I'll take up with decent eating habits. But he has known boys he has had to reject because they had been at bad eating tricks for a longer time. You can bet I'm going to follow the surgeon's advice after this."

Four out of this squad of candidates were rejected by the examining surgeons. Geroldstone remained sulky, with an air of bravado; the other three young men were so downcast that all their companions were heartily sorry for them. The hospital orderly marched back to the adjutant's office those who had been rejected, while another orderly appeared and led those who had passed the surgeons to the cadet barracks.

"This begins to look like the real thing," murmured Dick as

they neared the barracks.

Now this group were taken to the room of the cadet officer of the day, Lieutenant Edwards. Beside the cadet lieutenant's desk stood Cadet Corporal Brayton.

To the cadet officer of the day each of the candidates gave his name and home address, which were entered in a book.

"Brayton, take Prescott and Holmes to room number -, will you?" asked Mr. Edwards without looking up.

Dick and Greg followed their conductor outside and into another subdivision of barracks. Mr. Brayton kept on until he had reached the top flight, where he threw open a door.

"Step in here, Mr. Prescott and Mr. Holmes," ordered the cadet corporal stiffly. To the two new arrivals the corporal spoke as though he had conceived an intense dislike for these two boys. Later, Dick and Greg discovered that it was merely the way in which all candidates were treated by the cadet officers.

"You'll draw your bedding and other things presently," said Brayton coldly. "In the meantime you will remain here until you are ordered out. When you hear the order for candidates to turn out, obey without an instant's delay."

With that the corporal was gone, leaving the chums to gaze wonderingly about their new quarters.

Luxury? Not a bit of it. The room was severely plain. At one end was a double alcove, separated by a wall. In each alcove stood a bare-looking iron bedstead. There were two wash-bowls, two chairs and two desks that looked as though they had served the needs of generations of cadets. There was a window that looked out on the quadrangular area of barracks.

"Well, we're actually here, anyway," breathed Dick, his eyes

H. Irving Hancock

sparkling. "We're living in cadet barracks, and we're halfway through the ordeal of becoming new cadets at the wonderful old United States Military Academy!"

CHAPTER II

THE TYRANNY OF THE CADET CORPORAL

Dick hung up his coat and hat, and Greg did the same, for the heat was turned on and the room wholly comfortable as to temperature.

"I've heard," murmured Greg, "that fellows usually get most woefully homesick at West Point."

"Then they've no business to come here," retorted Prescott, with spirit. "Such tender ones won't make soldiers anyway."

"I suppose we shall be awfully looked down on at first," mused Greg aloud.

"Well, we can stand it," laughed Dick. "If we can't, we can't endure lots more of things that are ahead of us."

"Just now I could endure a good, filling meal," sighed Holmes comically.

"Yes?" laughed Prescott. "Then just press the button and the waiter will bring us the bill of fare. I understand that candidates are allowed to have their meals served in rooms. Although I believe it's forbidden for any candidate, or cadet, either, to eat his breakfast in bed."

"Quit your 'kidding,'" begged Greg.

"I don't know that the authorities will bother to feed us, anyway, until we've passed and it's known that we are going to stay and be cadets," laughed young Prescott, feeling around his belt-line, for he, too, was hungry.

"Candidates turn out promptly!" rang, from below, a voice full of military command.

Greg was in the middle of a comforting yawn and stretch. He dallied to finish it, but Dick, snatching down his overcoat and hat, was already out on the landing and racing below, while behind him floated the advice:

"Come on, Greg! Get a boost on!"

"Get along there, beasts," commanded a cadet corporal in the lower hallway sternly. "This is no sleeping match!"

Out in the yard several candidates had already run. Some of these young men at home, had been accustomed to being waited on by mothers and sisters. Yet here, in the seemingly freezing and hostile air of the Military Academy, these same young men were fast learning that everything has to be done by one's self, and at steam-engine speed.

"Mr. Danvers, come with me, and I'll place you as right guide," called Cadet Brayton with the air and tone of a budding military martinet.

Candidate Danvers followed meekly. Brayton looked at the lad's stooping shoulders with frigid, utter disapproval.

"Mr. Danvers, take your hands out of your pockets, sir."

"All right," laughed Mr. Danvers, obeying, and trying to laugh nonchalantly. "Anything to please."

"Don't address a superior officer, sir, unless he addresses you in a way to make a reply necessary. And when you do address a

Superior officer, or any other cadet or candidate on official business always add 'sir.'"

Danvers nodded, but the nod Cadet Corporal Brayton ignored by turning on his heel and stepping, with a magnificently military air and carriage, over to another luckless candidate.

When ordered, the candidate fell in next to Mr. Danvers. Then the other anxious youngsters fell into line.

"Candidates turn out promptly!" sounded snappily in another part of barracks.

Another lot of newcomers began to tumble downstairs and out of doors with feverish haste, to be confronted by another cadet corporal who awaited them.

"Never mind that other squad!" admonished Cadet Corporal Brayton sharply. "Favor me with your whole attention. Now, then, listen, and do each thing as I tell you. Button your jackets and overcoats all the way down! Stand erect, with your heels together, and your toes pointing out at an angle of sixty degrees. Stand erect. Throw your shoulders back, your chests out and hold your heads up. This is called 'the position of the soldier.' Stand as I do."

Corporal Brayton favored his awkward squad with a profile view of himself, as he took the exact position of a soldier. How the anxious candidates wished they really could stand as this handsome young son of Mars did! To them it seemed impossible ever to acquire such truly military carriage. They did not realize that, between drills, gymnasium work and the setting-up drills, they would, in a few weeks, be hard to distinguish in elegance and perfection from their present instructor.

"Not quite so much like an ostrich, Mr. Prescott!" rasped out Corporal Brayton severely.

Dick flushed painfully, all the more so because he heard one of the other candidates snicker.

"Stop that laughing, Mr. Danvers!" commanded Corporal Brayton.

Greg, in trying to get the right position, had so exaggerated it that now he found himself trembling from the strain of trying to maintain that position.

"What ails you, Mr. Holmes!" demanded Brayton, with withering scorn.

"I - I was trying to get the right position, sir," stammered Greg, reddening.

"That isn't the position of even a respectable dromedary, Mr. Holmes," rejoined the cadet corporal crisply.

Then he poured a storm of refined abuse upon Greg. It wasn't intended entirely for Greg, but for the benefit of all the awkwardly standing green candidates. Not a word in Brayton's remarks went beyond the limits of strict military propriety, yet every word cut.

"My, but I'd like to fall out and give this fellow a licking!" muttered Greg to himself.

"Mr. Holmes," observed Cadet Corporal Brayton dryly, "clenched fists do not go with the position of the soldier. Let your hands fall naturally at your sides, each little finger resting against the seam of the trousers, or where you judge the seam to be."

Again the blood shot up to the roots of Greg's hair, suffusing his face. But Mr. Brayton had already turned to another candidate whom he found in a ludicrously bad position. After some minutes of this attempt to instruct the candidates in the seemingly simple matter of standing correctly, Brayton gave the welcome order to rest.

By this time four other awkward squads were at the same work.

"I wish we had our uniforms," whispered Greg. "I'd feel better."

"I am glad I haven't a uniform yet," returned Dick in an equally low voice. "I realize how like a fool I'd look in it when I don't even know how to stand, let alone attempting to walk in a uniform. Just look at the magnificent carriage of the man that's drilling us!"

"I'd like to hammer him until he needed a carriage to get anywhere in," muttered Greg vengefully. "That corporal is a brute, without a vestige of good breeding."

"Then, for a fellow without breeding, he certainly carries himself like a king," retorted Dick. "At least, I don't believe any European prince has half as fine a carriage as Mr. Brayton."

"I wonder if they're all as bad as this corporal," demanded Greg. "Brayton is a tyrant in gray."

"Greg! Greg! Get a brace on yourself, old fellow," whispered Dick warningly. "This is only the morning of the first day, and we have before us months - years - of taking our medicine. Don't lose the gait even before you've got it. We came here to take our medicine and learn to be soldiers, didn't we?"

"Squad, attention!" rasped out Corporal Brayton, wheeling and once more favoring his own green lot with his whole regard.

Repeatedly he showed these new men how to stand, how to hold themselves and how to do it without appearing ridiculous. So crisp, so rapping and even decorously abusive

　　　　　　　H. Irving Hancock

was Mr. Brayton that the boys under his command at this moment would have gasped had they been told that Brayton was considered one of the easiest and best-natured of the cadet corporals. Brayton had his work to do - that was all. It was part of his own training to learn how to whip an awkward squad into time in the shortest possible order.

By-and-by all these anxious, even trembling, candidates were instructed in the mystery of marching a few steps at command, how to keep their alignment on the right guide, how to halt, the facings and all that.

"Now, we'll pass on to learning to count fours, and how to march off in column of fours," announced Brayton. "Squad halt!" he commanded hoarsely, in disgust, ere the young men had taken four steps. "Listen to me more attentively, and try more closely to follow orders!" glared the young corporal.

After that it seemed as though Cadet Corporal Brayton could have no other aim in life than to drive his squad of candidates away from West Point. At almost every move through the drill he berated them caustically, though in such faultless military language of reproof as to keep him from censure.

"Dismissed," glared Brayton at last. "The candidates will go to their rooms until summoned again."

Dick and Greg both felt stiff in the legs. Their backs ached from the long-continued drilling in what was yet, to them, the rigor of near-military carriage. Both chums toiled up the stairs to their bare room.

"Oh, you brute!" muttered Greg, standing in the middle of the room and shaking his fist in the direction of the area.

"Meaning - whom?" queried Prescott, with a wan smile.

"Whom could I mean but Brayton?" almost hissed young Holmes. "Why does that fellow hate us all so?"

"I'll tell you a secret, if you want to hear it," proposed Dick mysteriously.

"Please!" begged Candidate Holmes.

"Then I don't believe he does hate us."

"What?" gasped Greg incredulously.

"I don't believe he'd remember half our faces if he passed the members of his squad in the area right now," declared Dick.

"Then why does he persecute us so?" demanded Greg indignantly.

"I don't believe it is persecution," Dick continued.

"Then why, in the name of all that's kindly, does that fellow put us under the heel of hateful usage? Why must we submit to the tyranny of that cadet corporal?"

"It's the West Point way - that's all, I guess."

"Do you propose to submit to it?" challenged Greg.

"Yes," retorted Dick soberly. "I don't want to have to leave the Academy and go home stamped a failure."

"Neither do I," admitted Candidate Holmes in a more moderate tone. "But I wonder whether we have to stand so much nonsense from a petty young official like a mere corporal?"

"I'm afraid we do," nodded Dick. "Now, see here, Greg, can't you make a good guess as to why we're put through such a grilling?"

"I'll confess I can't see any human reason in it," declared Candidate Holmes.

"Why, what did we come here to learn to be?"

"Soldiers."

"Are we soldiers yet!"

"Of course not," Greg admitted.

"Do you think these people at West Point have time to coax and pamper us along!"

"Probably not. But can't they - or can't that fellow Brayton - be decent with us?"

"Now, look right here," counseled Candidate Prescott wisely. "We want to be soldiers, but as yet we're only ignorant, unregenerate, untaught young cubs. To the older cadets we must seem like pitiful beasts."

"No, we don't,"' sneered Candidate Holmes. "We don't seem anything at all. No cadet here, unless he's obliged to notice us, even looks at us. We're less than nothing."

"That's true," nodded Dick thoughtfully. "And I'll wager it will be pretty nearly as bad all the time we're plebes. Now brace up, Greg. Remember what a small fraction of nothing you are, and be thankful for the severe handling by Brayton, which may eventually transform us into at least pretty fair imitations of soldiers."

Outside a drum was sounding. It was mess call, but neither candidate knew it. Almost immediately, however, Brayton's rousing voice rang up through the subdivision:

"Candidates turn out promptly!"

"There's our slave-driver once more," frowned Candidate Holmes.

Dick, as he raced down the stairs, remembered to button his coat down its entire length. Greg forgot. As he darted through the doorway to the porch overlooking the area he found Corporal Brayton's gaze fastened upon him in severe displeasure.

"Mr. Holmes, button your coat, sir!"

Reddening and frowning, too, it must be admitted, Greg obeyed.

"All candidates will pass quickly through the north sally port and make formation," continued the cadet corporal.

Here the entire uniformed cadet corps was forming, facing the plain. At the extreme left of the line a cadet lieutenant, two sergeants and four cadet corporals busied themselves with forming the candidates and alternates in line. When the word was given the cadet corps wheeled to the right and marched off in column of fours, quite a splendid model of military precision.

Somehow the un-uniformed greenhorns managed to turn into column of fours, though some of the bewildered boys forgot to which four they belonged and there was some confusion.

Behind the superb cadet corps, toiled along these all but hopeless candidates and alternates, scores and scores of them - every fellow of them feeling more awkward than his nearest neighbors in the line. Badly out of step was this green material. Some of the boys slouched as they walked along; others shuffled. Their appearance was enough to dishearten a trained soldier.

But at last all these green ones were marshaled to seats in the great dining hall at cadet mess. There, in a fine dinner, they forgot, momentarily, many of the discouragements of the forenoon.

In the afternoon came a lot more of drilling of awkward squads by other cadet corporals. Greg soon found, under the tender mercies of another corporal, why Brayton was considered "easy."

These cadet corporals are all members of the yearling class, the class directly above the plebes. As corporals these members of the yearling class get their first direct experience in military command.

Later in the afternoon all candidates were notified that academic examinations would begin at eight o'clock the next morning in the Academic Building.

And now the candidates began to shiver! "Bad" as the start had been, they hoped, to a man, that they would pass these academic examinations. To fail meant to return home, the dream of being a cadet shattered!

"Ugh!" muttered Greg, rubbing his hands in quarters. "Br-r-r! Dick, I'm afraid I'm scared cold!"

Prescott smiled, but he, too, was worried over the coming mysteries of the academic examinations, which he had heard were uncommonly [Transcriber's note: word missing].

CHAPTER III

THE "LUCKY" ONES TAKE UP THE NEW LIFE

Candidate Prescott did not take the best examination by any means, but he got through without discredit in any branch.

A number of these candidates had spent the last year or so at some "prep." school that made a specialty of preparing young men for West Point and Annapolis.

Greg did fairly in English, quite well in history, geography and arithmetic; in algebra, through sheer nervousness, young Holmes barely escaped going short.

Nearly twoscore of the candidates failed utterly. These went sorrowing home, giving their alternates a chance to enter the corps in their places.

Soon after the results had been declared, the young men who had passed went over to headquarters. There they signed a statement to the effect that they entered the Military Academy with the consent of their parents or guardians, and bound themselves to serve in the Army at least eight years, unless sooner discharged. These new young men were then formally and impressively sworn into the service of their country. They were now cadets, even if only new plebes.

Why "new" plebes! Because, under the new system, with candidates admitted in March, there is still a "plebe" class

H. Irving Hancock

above them who remain plebes until commencement in June. Hence the distinction between old and new "plebes."

In the presence of all plebes the yearlings and other upper class men keep themselves loftily apart, except when compelled to drill the plebes or perform other military or other official duties with plebes.

The plebe, old or new, is still but a "beast" - a being unfitted for intimate contact with upper class men. The plebe is not an outcast. He is merely fifteen months on probation with his upper class comrades. Unhappy as the lot of the freshman is at some of our colleges, the plebe at West Point is of far less importance in the eyes of the upper classes.

Early every morning cadet corporals marched squads of new plebes out into the open and put them through the mysteries of the Army "setting-up" drills. These drills are effective in giving the new man, in an almost marvelously short time, the correct military carriage and physical deportment. Between these and the squad, platoon and company drills, it is truly wonderful how rapidly the new cadet begins to drop his former awkwardness.

The new plebes had now drawn their uniforms and rapidly learned the care of these parts of the soldier's wardrobe. They were also taught the proper occasions for wearing each article of uniform.

Academic studies had now begun in earnest too. The idea in requiring cadets to begin in March instead of in June, as formerly, is that they may have three months in which to become accustomed to the fearfully exacting requirements of study and recitation in force at West Point.

It was a proud day for all these new plebes when they "drew" their rifles and bayonets and began the laborious study of the manual of arms.

One after another, as fast as they were sufficiently proficient, the new plebes were sent into one of the companies into which the Corps of Cadets is divided.

Cadet Prescott entered D Company four days before Greg Holmes was assigned to the same company. Dick's success indeed spurred Greg on to new efforts, although poor young Holmes had felt that he was working as hard already as human flesh could endure.

Early in April nearly all of the new plebes had joined their companies. It was a wholly new, revolutionized life.

Many of the new plebes had come from homes of luxury, where servants had abounded.

But here at West Point former social lines had no significance, unless it was to invite trouble down upon the head of any new cadet who felt inclined to be priggish.

No cadet had a servant, nor could he engage anyone to perform any of his own duties for him.

Each cadet in the entire corps rose at the tap of a drum - "reveille" - at 5.45 A.M.

At the first sound of reveille every young man sprang from his bed. Then followed hasty but orderly dressing and the making of the toilet. The cadet must be spick and span.

Incidentally, but promptly, he fell to policing. The room must be in order, and the bed made up exactly in accordance with the regulations on the subject. All clothing must be hung as prescribed in the regulations. A match end or a scrap of paper on the floor brought reprimand and demerits.

"Policing" is the orderly care of quarters. At 6.20 police call sounded on the drum outside in the area. Then came a swift but all-seeing inspection of every occupied room in barracks.

Swiftly, indeed, was this done, for at 6.30 the tap of the drum sounded mess call for breakfast. The cadet corps formed outside the north sally port and marched to breakfast.

About seven o'clock breakfast ended. The corps marched back to barracks and was dismissed.

By 7.15 every young man was hard at work, "boning" hard over the studies in which he must recite during the forenoon. He "boned" until 7.55. Then, in his own appropriate section, he marched off to the Academic Building, remaining in the section room, under the instruction or quizzing of some officer of the Army until 9.20.

Now the new plebe, like the cadets of all classes, marched back to his room. At his desk he studied until summoned at 10.55 for the second recitation of the day, in some other subject.

At 12.10 he was dismissed from this second period of recitation, but 12.20 found the young man in dinner formation. From this mid-day meal the cadet reached barracks at 1.10. Now he had some time with which to do as he pleased; to be exact, he had fifteen minutes. At 1.25 the freshman marched off to recitation in English, history or French. At 2.30 the cadet found himself back in his room, forced to study, as few young men ever study in civil life, until 3.30.

From 3.30 to 6.25 P.M. the plebe was allowed to do as he pleased with his time, provided that in so doing he broke none of the regulations. He might amuse himself in various ways. He was at liberty to go over to the library, to read, for instance; he might call at officers' houses on the post on Saturday or Sunday afternoon if invited; he was at liberty to take a walk - within cadet limits. Or, if he felt the need of something really "wild" in the way of diversion, the lucky plebe was permitted to go over to the Academic Building and examine the mineralogical or geological collection!

As a matter of fact, the plebe who in most instances was doing badly with the great amount of study and recitation required of him, was likely to spend most of his afternoon leisure in "boning" the studies in which he was deficient or which he found difficult to master.

At 6.25 came the call for supper formation. That meal was through at about seven in the evening. Then came study time, lasting until 9.30 in the evening. At 9.30 the plebe was at liberty to turn down his mattress and go to bed, if he felt tired enough; if not, he was at liberty to study a little longer.

At 10.30, however, taps sounded on a drum just inside the north sally port. Now Mr. Plebe was obliged to turn out his light, instanter, and be in bed against the visit of the subdivision inspector, an upper class cadet, immediately afterward. If Mr. Plebe failed to be in bed he was reported - "skinned" - and punished accordingly.

In between there were always the drills, the gymnasium work, inspections, guard mount for each plebe about once a week after he had been admitted to the ranks of the battalion.

To the boy fresh from home it is a fearfully hard lot at first. That it can be lived through and endured, however, is proved by the fact that about six out of ten of the cadets who enter at West Point manage to graduate, and go forth into the Army, splendid specimens of physical and mental manhood. Very few of the cadets who fail at West Point and are dropped go away from the Military Academy without a mist before their eyes.

The plebes at West Point are not ostracized by the upper class men. These new men are merely "kept in their places" with great severity, and without any encouragement whatever. If the plebe can't stand it, then he is plainly not of the stuff to make a soldier. If he does stand it, he goes on into the upper classes, one after another, graduates and is commissioned by the President as a second lieutenant in the United States Army.

H. Irving Hancock

It is a hard ordeal, that fellowship of "nothingness" during the first portion of the West Point course.

Homesickness is the worst ailment of the new cadet. Day by day he grows more homesick until it seems to him that he simply cannot endure the Military Academy for another twenty-four hours.

One afternoon, while taking a walk as a relief from too hard application to his mathematics, Cadet Dick Prescott stumbled upon some news that made him open his eyes very wide.

"Well, of all things!" he growled to himself.

Then he walked faster.

"Greg must hear of this," muttered the new plebe.

Going down the street at military stride, Cadet Prescott turned in at the north sally port, stepped briskly along one of the walks, bounded up the steps and in at the outer door of the subdivision in which he dwelt.

Up the stairs with considerable speed went Cadet Prescott, still revolving in his mind the news upon which he had stumbled.

"What on earth will Greg think?" throbbed the new plebe.

In a very short time Prescott's hurrying feet carried him to the door of his room on the top floor. The door yielded as Dick put his hand to the knob.

"Greg, what do you think?" whispered Dick breathlessly, as he went quickly into the room and toward his roommate, who sat bent over his study table.

The very attitude was unmilitary - a fact that struck Prescott suddenly.

Then Greg, hearing his roommate's voice, raised his head somewhat and wheeled about in his chair.

What a woebegone face Cadet Gregory Holmes presented!

"Greg, what on earth is the matter?" demanded Dick, halting short and staring hard.

"I can't help it," replied Greg miserably, shaking his head.

"Can't help what?" demanded Dick thunder-struck.

"I can't help what I've gone and done. I had to do it!" cried Greg, with sudden fierceness in his tone.

"What you've done?" echoed Dick. "Well, what have you gone and done, anyway, old fellow? Does it stop anywhere short of murder - or lying?"

For in the West Point code of honor lying ranks very nearly as bad as murder.

"I guess perhaps it isn't quite as bad as either," smiled Greg wanly. "However, I couldn't help doing it."

He rose to his feet, a bit unsteadily, leaning one hand on his study desk.

Greg's hair was a bit awry, as though he had run his hands many times through it in some mood of desperation. This, in itself, was in defiance of West Point traditions for the personal neatness of the cadet.

"You still have me altogether in the dark, Greg," murmured Dick wonderingly.

"You'll lose all respect for me, Dick," went on Greg miserably.

"Then it must be something awfully bad that you've done,"

retorted Dick, opening his eyes wider than ever.

Without another word Greg reached to his desk, picked up a sheet of paper and in silence passed it over to his comrade.

Dick read with a gathering of his eyebrows. Then gradually a look of anger shot into his clear eyes.

"Greg Holmes," uttered the other cadet indignantly, "you're a disgrace to your native town of Gridley!"

"Well, what are you going to do about it!" demanded Greg almost defiantly.

"Do?" retorted Cadet Prescott. "I believe I'll thrash you - just for being a disgrace to our native place!"

Not intending anything of the sort, but merely as a dramatic expression of his rage, Dick doubled one fist, advancing upon Holmes.

At that instant the door was flung open. Cadet Lieutenant Edwards, of the first class, strode into the room.

Instantly both cadets straightened, where they were, standing at "attention," as required to do when a superior officer entered their quarters.

"What is this?" demanded Cadet Lieutenant Edwards, though betraying no more than official curiosity in his tone. "Have I entered just in time to prevent a fight!"

"No, sir," replied Cadet Prescott.

"Then what!"

"Sir," responded Cadet Prescott, "I wish to report my room-mate, Mr. Holmes, for writing this letter!"

Dick held out the sheet of paper, which the cadet lieutenant scanned earnestly.

H. Irving Hancock

CHAPTER IV

GREG'S CASE OF "BLUES"

Only a moment did Mr. Edwards need for the reading of Greg's note. Then the cadet lieutenant frowned at Dick.

"Mr. Prescott, what do you mean by perpetrating a poor-spirited joke under the guise of making an official communication?"

In an instant Dick saw clearly that be had made a military mistake.

"I beg your pardon, sir," he said meekly.

"This may all be a joke to you, Mr. Prescott," went on the cadet officer dryly, "but I presume it is none whatever to Mr. Holmes."

As he hadn't been addressed, Greg did not venture to answer. He stood rigidly at attention, though both he and Dick were flushing.

The paper that Mr. Edwards now held in his hand read as follows:

"To THE SUPERINTENDENT,"

"THE UNITED STATES MILITARY ACADEMY."

"Sir: I have the honor herewith to tender my resignation as a cadet in the United States Military Academy, the same to take effect immediately. I have the honor to be, sir,"

"Very respectfully,"

"GREGORY HOLMES."

"So that's the way you feel about it, is it, Mr. Holmes?" questioned the cadet lieutenant, after a second glance at the paper.

"Yes, sir," replied Greg.

"This is the fourth letter of the kind that I've seen this week," continued Mr. Edwards stiffly, though a curious smile played about the corners of his mouth. "I presume that two or three dozen, at least, of the same sort have been written by the new plebes. Mr. Holmes, do you know what was done with the other letters of resignation that I saw?"

"No, sir."

"Their writers tore them up," went on the cadet lieutenant stiffly. "Now, Mr. Holmes, if you persist in believing that you want to send this letter in to the superintendent, then I think it will be the best thing you can do; for if you still persist in wanting to resign, then you haven't manhood enough, anyway, to make a fit brother-in-arms for the comrades in your class."

This was severely said. Greg paled under the verbal thrashing.

"If you really wish to send in this letter," continued Mr. Edwards, "you have a perfect right to do it, Mr. Holmes."

"May I speak, sir?" asked Greg when the cadet lieutenant ceased talking, but remained looking fixedly at the new plebe.

"Proceed," replied Mr. Edwards.

"May I have that letter, sir?"

The cadet lieutenant handed it back without a word.

"May I - may I -"

"Out with it, Mr. Holmes."

"May I handle this letter at once in the way that I now wish, sir?"

"You may."

Greg, his face again flushing painfully, tore the sheet into small bits, turning and tossing them into his waste basket. Then he again wheeled, standing at attention.

"Stand at ease, mister," ordered Mr. Edwards, dropping out of his official tone and manner. "Now, mister, will it do you any good if I explain a few little things about life here at West Point?"

"I shall be very glad, indeed, sir, if you will be good enough," replied Greg rather shamefacedly.

"In the first place, mister," went on the cadet lieutenant, sitting, now, with one leg thrown over the corner of Greg's desk, "the homesickness that has hit you touches every other man who comes here. It's a mighty hard-working life here, and I'll admit, mister, that it's very cheerless during the plebe year.

"You think you are looked down upon, and regarded as being beneath contempt, mister. That sort of treatment for a plebe is believed to be necessary here. Grant got it; so did Sherman; so did Sheridan. George Washington would have been treated in just the same manner had there been a West Point for him to go to.

"It isn't because of what we upper class men think of you. It's because of what we're waiting to find out. I don't know anything about your connections in your home town. You may have been a great fellow there. You may, for all I know, have had a home of wealth, luxury and refinement. Your father may be a man of great importance in the nation. I don't know anything about that, and I don't care about it, either, mister. From the moment you start in at West Point, you start your life all over again, and you stand on nothing but your own merits. We don't know how much merit you have, and we shan't know until you've gone through with your plebe year and have proved whether you're a man or not. If we find, a year from this coming summer, that you're a man, we'll welcome you into the heartiest comradeship of all the corps. Mister, I've said a lot more to you than most upper class men would waste the time to say. Choose your own course, and prove where you stand."

Then Cadet Lieutenant Edwards turned around to Cadet Prescott with a look that made that Gridley boy feel rather uncomfortable.

"As for you, mister, never again, while you're a plebe, be so b.j. (fresh) as to try a joke with an upper class man. If there's one thing, mister, that gets a plebe into three times as much trouble as any other thing, then it's b.j.-ety!" (freshness).

Of a sudden the cadet lieutenant returned to his feet, resuming all the dignified demeanor of the cadet officer on duty.

Instantly Dick and Greg stood once more at "attention" until Mr. Edwards had turned on his heel and left the room.

"Hm!" murmured Dick, as they heard the lieutenant's retreating footsteps. "We've both had a jolly good lesson."

"You didn't do much," muttered Greg shamefacedly. "I wouldn't feel so bad about a call down over a bit of ordinary b.j.-ety. I was scorched and withered for being a cold-foot and a quitter - and I deserve it all, and more!"

"I'm glad you see that, old Gridley!" murmured Cadet Dick heartily. "Now, Greg, you won't write another letter of resignation, will you?"

"Not if I die of homesickness and melancholy!" muttered Greg, clenching his hands.

"Now, after letting you in for an awful verbal flogging," smiled Dick curiously, "I'll let you into a secret. I wrote a letter of resignation, too."

"When?" gasped Cadet Holmes amazed.

"Two days ago," confessed Dick. "I read it through six times before sending it to the superintendent."

"You didn't - send it to the superintendent?" gasped Greg.

"No; because I also tore it to fine bits before sending it to headquarters - and so the letter never reached the one to whom it was addressed," laughed Cadet Prescott. "Now, look here, Greg. Admit that you were a prize simpleton, just as I was. Let's start anew - with a bang-up motto. This is it: 'A Gridley boy may die, but resign - never!'"

Dick struck such a dramatic attitude that both poor young plebes began to laugh heartily.

"Oh, and now for the news that brought me back here hotfoot," ran on Prescott glibly. "Greg, you never could guess who's here at West Point."

"The President, or the Chief of the General Staff?" asked Holmes slowly.

"Oh, pshaw, no! They don't either one amount to as much as the fellow I'm talking about thinks he amounts to."

"Whom did our Senators appoint to the Academy?" asked Prescott after a pause.

"Me," admitted Greg, again turning red.

"Well, whom did the other Senator appoint!"

"A fellow named Spooner, who came here and 'fessed out' cold (failed badly) on the academic exam," Greg responded.

"Who was Spooner's alternate!" persisted Dick.

"I don't believe I remember," Greg replied slowly.

"No; and that was because neither you nor I ever knew. Spooner's alternate was - Bert Dodge!"

"What? Bert Dodge, of Gridley?" demanded Cadet Holmes astonished.

"That very chap," Prescott admitted. "When Spooner went home, after 'fessing out' here, Bert Dodge, who hadn't appeared, was ordered by wire to report at once, or have his name stricken out. Bert's physician wired the War Department that the young fellow was ill, though the illness would not delay him more than a few days. So Bert was given a brief grace. Well, sir, I've just learned that Dodge reported at the adjutant's office this morning. He got by the surgeons bounding, and to-morrow he sits down at his 'writs.' (written examinations) in the Academic Building."

"I wonder if that fellow will pass," cried Greg wonderingly.

"Oh, I rather think he'll make it easily," replied Dick, seating himself at his own desk. "Bert wasn't a fool at his studies. He spent more than three years at Gridley High School, and since then has had a school year and a half at one of the finest prep. schools in the country. Oh, I guess he'll get through all right."

"So we've got to have him here for a comrade!" sighed Greg disgustedly, as he picked up his text-book on English.

CHAPTER V

CANDIDATE DODGE IS CRITICAL

Both cadets had studied for ten minutes perhaps, when a knock sounded at their door.

The very unusualness of this caused both youngsters to look around, then at each other.

Had it been any cadet officer making an inspection - as was likely to happen at any minute of the waking day - he would have come straight into the room. And any other cadet, after knocking, would have followed this by opening the door and stepping inside.

Rap-rap! sounded again.

"Oh, come in," called Dick.

The door opened. Bert Dodge, dressed in the height of the prevailing fashion, looked inside.

"May I come in?" he called, in what was meant for a cordial, friend-from-home voice.

"Oh, yes, come in," sighed Dick wearily.

"That's not quite the welcome I might have expected from you two," muttered Bert, as he opened the door and stepped into the room. "Fellows, you're at West Point now," proceeded Bert Dodge pompously, "and this is a place where social points count tremendously, as I guess you've found out by this time. Now, you two may be all right, and I guess you are," admitted Bert condescendingly, "but you're just the sons of commoners, while my father is a wealthy man, a banker and a leader in society. So I guess you can quickly understand that I'm going to cut a good deal wider swath here than you two fellows put together."

Greg Holmes, who had been following Dodge with a gradually widening grin of amazement, now burst into a hearty laugh.

"Well, what's so awfully funny!" demanded Bert.

"You - you - social swell!" exploded Greg hilariously. "Oh - wow!"

"Oh, enjoy yourself in your own way," retorted Bert in decided anger, "but you'll soon find out."

Then looking about the room, he remarked, going on a new tack:

"I must say, you fellows are rather badly provided for showing the social courtesies here. You haven't even a chair for a guest."

"Plebes are allowed only two chairs to a room," remarked Dick, rising and pulling forward his own chair. "Take mine. I'll sit on the corner of my table."

"There's just one chair in my room," continued Bert, as he seated himself. "That's one reason I want to see the janitor, or steward, or whoever the fellow is. I'm going to tell him to put in a decent allowance of chairs."

Greg Holmes went off into another fit of laughter.

"Janitor? Steward?" sputtered Holmes. "Whew! That's great!"

"There are no such servants here, Dodge," Dick explained. "In fact, every cadet has to learn to wait on himself in nearly everything. A plebe, too, has to learn to be content with whatever he has given him. If he even makes any talk about it he is called b.j. A cadet who is found guilty of b.j.-ety has to put in all his spare time learning to walk on one ear."

"Do you mean to say you've been made to swallow stuff like that?" demanded Dodge, looking at Prescott in tall disdain. "Oh, well, you may be inclined to submit to such treatment, but I know who I am, and I'm not going to stand for any nonsense here. What's the matter with you, Holmes? Are you ill?"

For Greg's face, in his efforts to stifle his mirth, had become violently purple.

"I don't suppose you'll take advice, Dodge," continued Dick. "If I thought you only could do it I'd advise you to walk mighty slowly here, keep your lips together and not say a word until you've learned a lot."

Dick had risen and was standing, unconsciously, in an attitude that showed off, in his natty cadet uniform, all the strength and grace of his fine and now well set-up young figure. But Bert, with a desire to put this other fellow "back where he belonged," remarked casually:

"Prescott, I don't just like the fit of your coat. Who's your tailor? I want to get a different one. I'm going in for some of the swellest-fitting uniforms that any tailor around here can turn out."

Greg, who had managed to breathe naturally for the last minute, now struggled with another of his purple-faced paroxysms.

"I didn't think to ask who my tailor was," Prescott replied quickly. "In fact, I don't think I would have been told if I had asked. You see, every cadet here has to take just what clothes are issued to him at the cadet store. That's the rule for all cadets here."

"Do you mean to tell me that I've got to wear 'hand-me-downs'?" demanded Bert Dodge angrily. "Save that sort of stuff for fellows who'll believe it."

It was plain that, if Bert Dodge had dropped in with any intention of being neighborly and from-home, he had rapidly forgotten his plan.

Neither Dick nor Greg had any reason for being fond of the fellow, even if he had once been a schoolmate at Gridley High School. Bert, son of Theodore Dodge, a Gridley banker, was an unpardonable snob. Readers of the High School Boys Series will recall how Bert had been one of the leaders in the "sorehead" secession from the football ranks at Gridley High School. That movement failing in its purpose, Bert had afterwards provoked Dick Prescott into striking him, and had then had Dick arrested for assault. The suit had failed, and Bert was rebuked by the court. Much more of the feud that young Dodge had attempted to wage upon Prescott and his High School chums was fully narrated in "THE HIGH SCHOOL LEFT END."

It was nearly a year since Bert had seen either of these chums. That he had entered their room in cadet barracks full of the purpose of impressing them with his new importance was at once plain.

Dick was just beginning to find the atmosphere oppressive when the door was pushed quickly open after the faintest suggestion of a knock.

The newcomers were Cadets Pratt and Judson of the yearling class, known already among the plebes as two of the worst hazers.

"Attention!" hissed Pratt, as he strode into the room.

Neither of the visitors being a cadet officer, Dick and Greg were not obliged to stand at attention.

However, neither new plebe was foolish enough to argue the matter. Dick and Greg took the pose ordered and at once.

"Mister," demanded Pratt, turning upon Dick, "what is this cit. (citizen) doing in barracks?"

"Mr. Dodge is a candidate, sir, quartered in this building, and he took it into his head to visit us."

"What are you doing on that chair, Candy?" demanded Judson, flashing an angry look at Bert.

"None of your business!" retorted Dodge.

"You'll stand at attention!" retorted Cadet Judson, gripping Bert by the collar and pulling him to his feet.

"That'll be about enough, Jud," warned Cadet Pratt in a low voice. "Remember, the fellow is nothing but a candidate."

"You fellows seem to think you're mighty important," sputtered Bert. "I'm not in the habit of associating with hoodlums!"

"Now, if that isn't the b.j.-est sunflower that ever grew in a farmyard," remarked Cadet Pratt, with a wink at Cadet Judson.

"If you're referring to me be a bit more careful in your witticisms," warned Dodge stiffly, "or I shall demand satisfaction."

"Oh, you're rather certain to get all the sat. you want, I imagine when you're a cadet," retorted Cadet Pratt dryly.

"But, Jud, our time is fairly running away from us, and we have yet other social calls to make. Our respectful farewells, misters."

Turning, straight and stiff as ramrods, Cadets Pratt and Judson marched from the room.

When their step was heard on the stairway Greg stepped over and closed the door.

"Well, you fellows are the meekest green apples that I ever saw," laughed Dodge scornfully. "You simply lay down and allowed those two military bullies to walk over you just as they chose. Do you expect to get through West Point like men, if you have no more self-pride than that?"

"I'm heartily glad you've joined us here, Dodge," murmured Greg artlessly. "You'll show us, by your own example, just how to stand up for our rights."

"Humph! I hope you'll be able to learn," grunted Bert, rising as he glanced at his watch.

Then he went on, a trace more amiably:

"I find I've got to go back to my room and prepare for supper. Now, fellows, we haven't always gotten along in the best shape at home. But here at West Point I suppose we all start life on somewhat of a new footing. I'm willing to let by-gones be by-gones if you don't presume altogether too much on coming from the same home town. Keep your places with me, and we'll try to go along on a somewhat pleasanter basis than in the past. Let us try to forget the past. Ta-ta, fellows. See you at the supper table."

Bert stalked out loftily, with a considerable appreciation of his condescension toward two fellows whom he had been wont, in past years, to call muckers.

"Hold me!" begged Greg hoarsely. "I'm going to have a fit. Oh, wow! Dick, just think of that poor b.j. lamb falling into the hands of the yearlings! What'll they ever do with him?"

"Greg, it has been hard enough on us to get used to the new ways at West Point. But we'll never mind anything during the rest of our plebedom. No matter what happens to us we'll just remember how much more is bound to happen to pompous old Dodge."

Dick returned to his table, picking up his text-book on French. Greg honestly tried to study, but every other minute he simply had to stop to laugh at the thought of Bert and his pompous ways.

Finally, when he could restrain himself no longer, Greg broke forth:

"Dick, old ramrod, no matter what happens to me, now I can stand it by thinking of Bert Dodge being here!"

"I hope he doesn't start his old tactics of making trouble," muttered Cadet Prescott.

"If he does, he'll have most of the trouble in his own possession," grinned Greg. "West Point is a place where manliness has the only real show."

"Yes, but a sneak can make an awful lot of trouble," sighed Dick. "Not that I mean to call Dodge a sneak, though. I am in hopes that he'll prove anything but that. From the minute that a fellow enters the Military Academy he starts in life all over again. So, remember, Greg, we won't be prepared to hate or distrust Dodge, and we'll lose a hand before we'll utter a word against him, based on anything that happened in the past."

"That's the square deal, and the West Point ideal," nodded Greg, who was rapidly forgetting the letter, the fragments of which were now in his waste basket. "Who knows but that, in this new atmosphere, Bert Dodge may turn out to be a man? West Point will do that very thing for him, if any new surroundings can."

As the battalion marched to supper that night Bert Dodge felt in his heart that hazing must already have started for him; for, being the only candidate left at West Point, and having no uniform as yet, Dodge was compelled to march, in his rather gay "cit." attire, at the extreme end of the battalion line.

Bert did not march quite alone, however.

Just behind him, majestic, unbending, lynx-eyed and exacting, marched Cadet Corporal Spurlock, who was known as the "worst" (strictest) of the Yearling cadet officers.

"Chest out, Mr. Dodge! Don't wobble so at the knees, sir! Can't you carry yourself straight? Take your chin away from your chest, Mr. Dodge. Try to keep step, sir. Follow my count - hep! hep! hep! hep! Mr. Dodge, you're out of step! When I call 'hep' put your left foot down, sir! But don't keep it down, sir!" added the exasperated cadet corporal in a furious undertone, as Bert came to a dead halt. "Mr. Dodge, try to exhibit something close to intelligence. Now, again, sir! Hep! hep! hep! hep!"

An Army officer stationed at the post drove by on a springboard. Three young women were with him. They saw and partly understood. The peal of laughter that floated back from them brought a flush to the face of the green, pestered candidate.

CHAPTER VI

IN THE HANDS OF THE YEARLING HAZERS

Under the hard grilling of cadet corporal Spurlock, Bert Dodge actually made a lot of progress within the next few days.

Dodge learned that, whenever addressing an officer, whether that officer were a cadet officer, or one of the Regular Army officers stationed at the Academy as instructors, he must add "sir" to every communication. He also learned that he must not address any superior officer unless first addressed by him.

Bert also picked up rapidly the knowledge that he was no better than anyone else, and of not a thousandth part of the importance of any upper class man.

Much of this the young man picked up from his new roommate, Tom Anstey, a soft-eyed, soft-voiced, helpful and sunny young man from Virginia. Anstey was one of the best-liked men in his class, but the new plebes at first held almost aloof from Dodge.

"Whatever you do," urged Anstey, "don't make the mistake of trying to cultivate the acquaintance of any of the upper class men."

"I've encountered two already," muttered Bert.

"Oh!" and Anstey smiled wonderingly.

"Pratt and Judson, of the yearlings," Dodge continued, then related what had happened in the room of Cadets Prescott and Holmes.

"I guess you're going to be in for it, presently, Dodge," nodded Cadet Anstey. "Mr. Pratt and Mr. Judson are known as two terrors."

"They don't want to try to pass any of their terror on to me," growled Bert.

Whereupon Mr. Anstey took his roommate in hand, gently and genially, and tried to make that new cadet - for Bert had passed his academic exams. without even a hint of trouble - understand how worse than foolish it would be to attempt to antagonize the upper class men.

"You come from the same place that Prescott and Holmes do, don't you?" asked Anstey, one afternoon, as the roommates rested from study.

"I'm glad to say I don't," replied Bert, almost brusquely.

"Oh!" nodded Anstey.

"I suppose we've got to be comrades, now, but I don't like that pair an over-lot," Bert explained.

"Odd! Most of the new plebes like Prescott and Holmes all the way up, and then all the way down again," murmured Anstey seriously. "For myself, I don't know any two fellows in the new lot that I like better."

"Oh, I guess they're all right in a good many ways," admitted Bert slowly. "Only we never managed to hitch - that's all. You asked me if I came from the same place. I used to live in Gridley, but I - er - well, I went away to Fordham to another school. My father had a summer place in Fordham, and he took up his voting residence in Fordham, though spending a good part of his winters in Gridley. That's how I'm credited to Fordham, not Gridley."

"Thank you for telling me," nodded Anstey. "I had just been wondering if it were not crowding things a bit to send three young men all from Gridley."

"I'm not only not from Gridley, but I came in as an alternate, anyway."

"How are you getting on with Corporal Spurlock?" asked Anstey.

"That fellow? Oh, hang him! Spurlock drives me wild. I came within a hair's breadth of applying to the commandant of cadets for a new instructor in drill. Only you told me that no heed would be paid to such a request from a new plebe."

"I should rather say not," grinned Anstey. "However, you'll be through the prelim. grind soon, and then you'll be admitted to a company in the battalion."

"I'm fitted for it now," growled Bert.

"You won't get into a company, though, until Corporal Spurlock reports you as fitted."

"That fellow is the most rascally tyrant I ever saw anywhere," growled Bert, picking up a text-book on mathematics.

By this time the season of outdoor drills and daily dress parade had arrived. This particular afternoon, however, in the latter part of March, a heavy, blinding snowstorm had come along. Cadets were nearly all in barracks, therefore, and those who had the most need were studying hard.

"I've boned math., boned French, boned English," muttered

Anstey, at last. "Now, I think I'll go over and bone Prescott and Holmes. Feel like going along with me!"

Bert frowned somewhat. He didn't care to "approve" of the two Gridley boys too much. But it was so deadly dull in this room that Dodge didn't care to be left alone, either.

"Oh, I'll go," nodded Dodge, closing a book with a snap and rising. "But I'd like it even better if you had some one else in mind to visit."

"You see," almost apologized Anstey, "I want to see Prescott and Holmes particularly because I've been talking over football with them, and they've been telling me a lot about their high school eleven that was right smart and interesting."

Bert said no more. If his ancient foes were going to tell Anstey about the old football days back in Gridley, then Bert feared they might be tempted to tell a lot that would bring up his unpopular share in those spirited old days.

"But Prescott and his shadow won't dare to say anything against me if I'm sitting right there in the room," muttered Bert to himself.

So he and Anstey presented themselves at Dick and Greg's door. Bert was almost amazed to find himself pleasantly greeted, but Dick and Greg were true to their decision to bury the hatchet of the past if possible.

It was nearly time to light the gas. In the fading light Anstey walked over to a window, watching the snow swirl down into the area outside. At West Point the snowstorms are famous for their severity.

"Hang it!" growled Anstey. "I don't suppose you can ever make a Virginian like myself grow to like this beastly winter weather. And I miss the drills and dress parade. Don't you?"

"Yes," nodded Dick. "I miss everything of an outdoor nature, when it is withheld from me."

"Oh, if you're missing outdoors just now, you might go out and keep on, within cadet limits, until you've tramped five miles," grinned the cadet from Virginia.

"If some of the upper class men found that we liked to be out in a snowstorm, I'm afraid they'd make us stand on our heads in a drift," laughed Cadet Holmes.

"Speaking of that," continued Anstey, wheeling about, "have any of you fellows run into real hazing as yet?"

"Not I," replied Prescott, with a shake of his head.

"Nor I," added Greg.

"It's a shame that we should be expected to put up with any such nonsense," growled Cadet Dodge belligerently. "Who are the yearlings that they should feel at liberty to rub our noses in the mud! We plebes ought to combine to put a stop to this outrage. Now, I'd like to see any smart year -"

"Eh!" called a voice, cheerily, as the door was thrust open. Yearling cadets Pratt and Judson stepped into the room.

Instantly three of the plebes present rose and stood at attention. Bert Dodge didn't.

"What has got into your sense of military manners, mister!" demanded Cadet Pratt, transfixing Bert with a haughty stare.

"What's wrong with my manners!" demanded Cadet Dodge.

"What's that!" cried Pratt.

"What's wrong with my manners!" repeated Dodge, though a bit more tractably.

"What?"

"What is wrong with my manners, sir!" Bert amended.

"That's just a shade better, mister," admitted Yearling Pratt. "But you are too sparing of your 'sirs,' mister. Now, answer me again, and use 'sir' after each word."

Plebe Dodge gulped hard, but Pratt and Judson were glaring at him. So he began:

"What, sir, is, sir, wrong, sir, with, sir, my, sir, manners, sir!"

"Mister, why didn't you stand at attention when we entered the room!"

"Because you're not -"

"What!" exploded Yearling Judson.

"Because, sir, you're, sir, not, sir, my, sir, superior, sir, officers, sir."

"Are we yearlings!"

"Yes, sir."

"And what are you!" demanded Cadet Judson, with infinite contempt.

"Only, sir, a, sir, plebe, sir."

"Mangy, unkempt, uncouth and offensive, are you not!"

Bert flared and swallowed hard, but he responded, very meekly:

"Yes, Sir."

"You're - what?"

"A, sir, mangy, sir, unkempt, sir, uncouth, sir, and, sir, offensive, sir, plebe, sir."

"Very true," nodded Mr. Pratt. "But, at least, mister, you have learned how to answer a yearling or any other superior, haven't you!"

"Yes, sir," Bert meekly assented.

"But there's one thing the poor beast doesn't know how to do yet," observed Mr. Judson, turning to his classmate. "He doesn't understand how to stand at attention when he is honored by a yearling's visit."

"Teach him - if you find that he's intelligent enough," advised Yearling Pratt.

"Turn down that mattress, mister," commanded Mr. Judson, pointing to Dick Prescott's iron cot.

Bert made the mistake of looking first at Cadet Prescott for permission.

"Now, mister, what makes you hesitate!" fumed Mr. Judson.

"It isn't my cot, sir," replied Dodge.

"What?"

"It, sir, is, sir, not, sir, my, sir, cot, sir."

"That has nothing to do with your orders. Turn down that mattress!"

Bert obeyed with great alacrity.

"Now, then, mister," ordered Yearling Judson, "get up on that mattress, and stand at attention upside down!"

It took Bert Dodge a few precious seconds to understand the full nature of the ignominious thing he had to do.

This was neither more nor less than to stand on his head on the mattress. He could rest his hands beside his head, at the outset, bracing his feet against the wall. So far it was not difficult. But -

"Don't you know the position of attention, mister!" demanded Cadet Pratt, with feigned anger. "Your hands should hang naturally at your sides, the little finger touching the seam of the trousers."

Now, in this inverted position the hands "hung" anything but "naturally" at the sides. In fact, Bert had to hold his hands up in the air in order to have the little fingers touch the seams of the trousers.

Standing on his head, in this fashion, without support, was something that taxed all of Mr. Dodge's athletic powers. He had to try over again, more than a half a dozen times, ere he achieved a decent performance of this gymnastic feat.

"Now, let us see how good a soldier you are, mister," commanded Yearling Pratt, turning around upon Plebe Anstey.

Anstey's cheeks were just a bit pale, from suppressed anger, but he speedily mastered this novel way of standing at attention, and did it to the satisfaction of the hazers.

Then Dick and Greg did it, and rather better than either of their predecessors. The old gym. and field work of training for the Gridley High School teams had hardened their muscles in a way that stood them in good stead now.

"Brace, mister!" commanded Yearling Judson, focusing his

gaze on smarting Bert Dodge.

Bert knew what that meant, from hearsay, and didn't pretend that he didn't. This time he took the position of attention on his feet, and then exaggerated the position by throwing his head and shoulders as far back as he could, standing rigidly in this latter position.

It isn't much of a thing to do, as far as taking the attitude goes. It is the length of time a plebe is kept at a "brace" that makes it count as an effective form of hazing. "Bracing" is generations old at West Point. The theory of upper class men has always been that bracing, long continued, fastens the principles of erect carriage upon a plebe, and teaches him, more quickly than anything else could, how to hold himself and to walk.

Dick, Greg and Anstey were likewise soon straining themselves in the "brace" attitude. And mighty funny these four hapless plebes looked as they stood thus, wondering when the hazers would let up on them. But Yearlings Pratt and Judson looked on grimly, warning any plebe as often as the offender showed a disposition to lessen the severity of his "brace."

How everyone of the four ached can be determined by the reader if he will take the full position of the brace, and hold it steadily for ten or fifteen minutes by a friend's watch.

Dodge began to wobble at last. Anstey was sticking it out pluckily, but knew his endurance must soon give out. Dick and Greg felt their back muscles and nerves throbbing. Yet neither Judson nor Pratt showed any intention of giving the command to stop.

Suddenly a quick step was heard in the hallway outside.

Anyone who has been at the Military Academy as long as had Pratt and Judson knew the meaning of that particular, swift step.

One of the "tacs.," as the tactical officers are called, was making an unscheduled tour of inspection. For an upper class man to be caught hazing, or for a plebe to be caught submitting, was equally dangerous to either yearling or plebe! It might mean dismissal.

CHAPTER VII

A SUDDEN GRIND AT MATH.

Had Dick's been the first door opened six cadets would have been instantly in serious trouble.

Fortunately the door across the corridor was the first to be opened, and the six on this side of the hallway heard another cadet's voice call quietly:

"Attention!"

It was, therefore, a tactical officer making an inspection.

At the United States Military Academy the superintendent, who has the local rank of colonel, is at the head of this government institution in all its departments.

Discipline, however, and training in tactics, comes within the especial province of another officer, known as the commandant of cadets, who ranks locally as a lieutenant-colonel, and who gets in closer touch with the cadet corps.

Under the commandant of cadets are several other Army officers, captains and lieutenants, who take upon themselves the numerous duties of which the commandant has oversight. These subordinate officers in the tactical department are known as tactical officers. The cadets call them "tac.s."

Each day one of these "tac.s" is in charge at the office of the commandant, which is in cadet headquarter's building, on the south side of the area of cadet barracks.

This officer, who is in charge for a full period of twenty-four hours, when his turn comes, is officially designated as the "officer in charge." Among the cadets he is privately referred to as the "O.C." In a similar way, in cadet parlance, the commandant himself is known as the "K.C."

Now, one of the numerous duties of the O.C., who is an Army officer and himself a graduate of West Point, is to make sudden, unexpected tours of inspection whenever the fancy - or the suspicion - seizes him.

Such an inspection need by no means extend through the whole of cadet barracks. It may, for that matter, be only to one subdivision, or even to a single floor or room of one subdivision. Yet record must be kept of such inspections, and of any offenses against discipline that may be discovered by such a flying visit.

A scrap of paper on the floor, a match end on a study table, any article of furniture or clothing out of its proper place, or any undress or untidiness on the part of a cadet, constitutes a breach of discipline, and must be reported and atoned for. Naturally, a case of hazing would be a most serious "delinquency," as breaches of discipline are termed.

Just what Captain Vesey, O.C., on this day, expected to discover through the present flying inspection will never be known. If he had tried Dick's door first. [Transcriber's note: missing text?]

But he didn't.

However, there was no chance whatever for Yearlings Pratt and Judson to retreat unseen. The door across the hall had been left open, and the tac. would be sure to detect their sudden departure.

Dick Prescott's first movement was to pounce upon his disordered bedding, swiftly folding over the mattress, and laying the bed clothing in the prescribed manner.

Then he tiptoed up to the dismayed Judson, whispering in that yearling's ear as he knowingly winked at Pratt:

"If I'm not too abominably b.j., sir, won't you please come to my table and help me bone math?"

It looked like a saving inspiration. As Dick slipped into his chair he signed to Bert Dodge to stand at one end of the table. Judson snatched up one of Dick's mathematical textbooks, opening to one of the first pages at random. Dick turned sideways in his chair, glancing up at the yearling with a rapt expression.

Yearling Pratt slipped into Greg's chair. Holmes and Anstey stood on either side of him. Pratt began rapidly to sketch out a problem that he chanced to remember from plebe year math.

Almost instantly the door swung open. Not one of the cadets happened to be looking in that direction. As Captain Vesey, the tac., white-gloved, stepped into the room he was just in time to hear Cadet Judson say:

"Perhaps if you were to work out a formula in algebra, mister, you would find the idea even more clear. But I think you understand it now."

"Yes, sir, thank you," replied Cadet Prescott.

"This is the way I would explain the problem," murmured Mr. Pratt, to Greg and Anstey. Just at that instant the yearling looked as though butter couldn't melt in his mouth.

Turning a bit, Pratt caught sight of the tac., who stood looking on as though transformed with wonder.

"Attention!" called Pratt at once.

All the others wheeled, Dick rising in order to do so. Six young men who looked intensely earnest over study, faced the O.C. respectfully.

Doubtless a bit taken back, certainly so if he had expected to find anything wrong, Captain Vesey took two steps into the room, glanced about him, then wheeled and walked out.

"I must be going now," uttered Yearling Judson a moment later. "Call on me again, once in a while, if you need any help in math."

"Thank you very much, sir," murmured Cadet Prescott respectfully.

"Coming along now, Pratt?" called Judson.

"Yes; I must be getting back to my own bone," replied Yearling Pratt.

It would have been out of the question for yearlings to thank plebes for a service such as had just been rendered. So the late hazers merely stepped from the room.

"Odd! Mighty queer!" muttered Captain Vesey to himself, as he unhooked his sword and stood it in a corner over in the O.C.'s office. "Mr. Judson and Mr. Pratt have a pretty bad reputation for hazing. And yet, when I come upon them, it is to find them helping the poor young greenhorns through the mazes of math. I wonder if that was a put-up job on me."

"Well you are a silly ninny, Prescott!" uttered Cadet Dodge disgustedly.

"Meaning - what?" asked Dick coolly.

"Those yearlings were just about caught redhanded."

"Yes."

"And you had to go to work and arrange amateur dramatics like a flash. So when the tac. pops in here, he finds those most estimable young ruffians conducting an innocent day school here!"

"Well?" demanded Prescott.

"Why didn't you leave it for that yearling couple to pull their own chestnuts out of the fire?"

"Because," replied Dick quietly, "I'm not going to be the means, if I can help it of having any man kicked out of this corps when he's as anxious to be a soldier as I am!"

"You're a ninny, just the same!" Bert decided.

"And you're a hopeless minority here, Dodge, so come along back to our room," broke in Anstey. "We've some boning of our own to do before the call sounds for supper formation."

Before the battalion of cadets marched to supper, through the heavy storm that night, the news of Dick Prescott's inspiration had traveled pretty firmly through the yearling class.

It is against all West Point traditions to make a hero of a plebe. Not a word of congratulation came to Cadet Prescott. It wouldn't even save the young man from being the victim of a lot of hazing pranks, for these inflictions were deemed necessary to the plebe's training. None the less, the incident, as it became known, caused the impression to spread that Cadet Prescott was a good fellow and that he was likely to prove a credit to the grand old United States Military Academy.

Hazing a thing of the past at West Point! The War Department and the authorities at the Military Academy have done all they could, and will continue to do all in their power to stamp out hazing.

Since the Congressional investigation in the early years of the present century, much has been done to cut down the rigor of hazing at West Point. General Mills stamped out much of it with iron vigor. Colonel Scott dealt many hard blows to the system. Other officers have bent their energies to the same problems. The way of the hazer is perilous nowadays. In a word, of late years hazing has been at a very low level at the United States Military Academy.

It is, however, a practical impossibility to stamp out hazing wholly in an institution where hazing has been one of the most cherished traditions through many generations of cadets.

The hazing of today is milder; there is less of it, and, with rare exceptions, it is less brutal. Yet hazing, in one form or another, will doubtless continue at West Point through the twentieth century as it did through the nineteenth.

The form of hazing has changed, if not the spirit. Sorely pressed by tac.s, and by other officers stationed at West Point, the yearlings, or second-year men, who do most of the hazing, have developed new forms of the ancient sport, and some of these forms may be carried on in actual sight of an Army officer without exciting his suspicions.

Where possible, some of the old-style forms of more innocent and purely mischievous hazing are retained. Where "necessary" new hazes are employed that are bound to tax the best efforts of disciplinary or other officers to detect.

Hazing is one of the diversions of men of mature age on the floor of the New York Stock Exchange. Even in the United States Senate there are recognized ways of hazing a new Senator who displays too little reverence for the traditions of that august body.

Then why hope to abolish hazing utterly at West Point?

CHAPTER VIII

DICK BONES TROUBLE

As May drew on towards June there was, among the yearlings, a noticeable falling off of interest in hazing. Every second-year man in the corps found himself much more interested in his standing in his studies than formerly.

Several of the yearlings had reason to feel acutely concerned over their standing in academic work. That some of them would be "found" and dropped from the corps on account of their deficiencies was almost a foregone conclusion.

So the warm nights of May found anxious young men in all the classes boning up to within a few minutes of the sound of taps.

Least anxious of all the cadets were the scores of new plebes. They had been required to report in March mainly that they might acquire the proper West Point habits of study and recitation before going into the summer encampment. Hence these new plebes were not to be treated very searchingly in the academic work.

One afternoon Greg, who had felt half ailing for twenty-four hours, went on sick report and walked to the hospital to consult the medical officer in charge.

Captain Goodwin looked Greg over and ordered him to

remain at hospital that night for observation and treatment, declaring that the young plebe would doubtless be all right by morning.

Cadet Prescott was alone in their room, boning hard, at about nine that evening, when a member of the cadet guard informed him that he was wanted by the O.C. It was only to make an explanation of something trivial that had occurred that afternoon.

As Dick rose, placing his desk in order, he decided to turn off the gas during his absence. This he did, then left the room.

Crossing the area he climbed the stairs to the office of the O.C. Pausing at the threshold, he saluted, then was bidden to enter.

Dick's report was quickly made. He was then permitted to return to quarters.

As Cadet Prescott threw open his door the room was in darkness, hardly any light entering from the hallway.

As Dick stepped into the room he was startled to see a dimly defined figure bending over his cot.

In the poor light it seemed to Prescott that the intruder wore the attire of a "cit."

Now, no civilian had any right in the room, nor in cadet barracks, for that matter. Prescott's first swift conclusion was that some scoundrel was there for wholly improper purposes.

"You rascal, I've got you!" exclaimed the plebe, crossing the room almost in a single bound.

Swift as a flash Dick laid hands on the intruder, dragged him back from the cot, wheeled him around and let drive a blow from the shoulder that caught the prowler on the nose and sent him to the floor.

"Let up, you b.j. plebe!" came a roar of smothered rage.

The body had fallen nearer the door, where the light from outside was stronger.

Dick noted, with a thrill of dismay, that the other was attired not in "cit." dress, but in the cadet gray.

"Hold on a minute," begged Prescott.

Striking a match he turned on the gas. As the light flamed up Dick saw Cadet Corporal Spurlock standing before him, quivering with rage.

"You b.j. plebe!" snarled Mr. Spurlock. "I'll take this out of you!"

"Certainly," replied Dick promptly. "But, first of all, I want to assure you that I didn't see the uniform. I thought I had discovered a cit. in here, and I knew no cit. could be here on any honest business."

"Bosh!" growled Spurlock, who was holding a handkerchief to a nose that was bleeding freely.

Cadet Prescott drew himself up, his eyes flashing.

"Pardon me, sir," returned Dick. "But you know, as well as I, sir, that a lie is impossible to a cadet."

It was a hard report to get around that a cadet had told a lie. At times cadets have been known to lie, but invariably, after detection, they have been "cut" and forced out of the corps. So lying is a rare occurrence, indeed, among the cadets.

"I'll make you settle for this, anyway," sputtered Cadet Corporal Spurlock.

H. Irving Hancock

"Very good, sir," Dick answered resolutely.

"You'll settle at once, too, mister, or as soon as I've stopped this flow."

"Very good, sir," Dick answered again. "But if I'm not too b.j., sir, in talking at all, I'll call your attention to that clock. There is just time for you to reach your quarters before taps sound."

Spurlock glanced hastily at the clock.

"You're right, mister," he admitted. "Then you may wait until you hear from me, mister."

With that Spurlock walked quickly from the room.

Dick examined his cot and found that Spurlock had been engaged in the humorous trick of placing some two score exploded caps from target-rifle ammunition under his under sheet.

"He wanted me to jump into bed and go down plump on all those caps, and then squirm there until after taps inspection," grinned Prescott as he swiftly removed the stuff. "It would have been a tough one, too - but now I guess I have a tougher proposition on my hands."

Prescott sighed a trifle as he hastily undressed, placing his clothing according to the regulations on the subject.

Just as he had finished taps sounded on the drum outside. Dick turned off his gas, bounded into bed and lay there as the door opened and the bull's-eye lantern of the subdivision inspector flashed into the room.

"All right here, sir, or accounted for," Dick remarked to the inspector, who hastily closed the door and hurried along on his rounds.

True to the medical officer's promise Greg was discharged from hospital the following morning, and permitted to report back to full duty.

"What's this I hear, Dick, old ramrod?" Greg demanded as soon as the chums were back in quarters from breakfast. "The news is flying around fast that Mr. Spurlock is going to call you out."

"I expect that he is," Dick admitted ruefully, and then told his chum all the details of the occurrence of the night before.

"Why, that doesn't strike me as fair excuse for a fight," Greg muttered. "You explained and apologized."

"Mr. Spurlock wouldn't accept any apology."

"Just the same," argued Greg, "I don't believe you have to fight, in this case. You can refuse, anyway, until the matter has been examined into by the scrap committee of the yearling class. Now, in view of the fact that you offered explanation and apology, I don't believe that the yearling scrap committee can hold you to any meeting with Mr. Spurlock this time. Let me handle this affair for you, old ramrod."

"Greg," rejoined Dick, laying an affectionate hand on his roommate's shoulder, "as long as I'm a new plebe I don't intend to try to dig out of any fight that an upper class man demands from me. Perhaps I could get the scrap committee to turn down Mr. Spurlock's desire - but I don't mean to do anything of the sort. I did all that I felt I could do consistently to stop the fight. Now it has got to come off, or else it will be because Mr. Spurlock has become more reasonable."

"He'll eat you up, that big fellow," mused Greg bitterly. "Mr. Spurlock is at least fifteen pounds heavier than you. He has had a year more of West Point gym work than you've had and he has the reputation of being pretty nearly the yearling champion in the ring."

"Of course I shall be thrashed," admitted Dick doggedly. "However, that probably won't do me any permanent harm. Besides, Greg, it's certain that I'll have to fight some yearling sooner or later, so I may as well take the dose now. Every plebe, I reckon, has to have one fight, anyway, with a yearling. It's a part of the system here, from all I can hear."

Rap-tap sounded at the door.

"Come in," called Dick, but the door opened just as he was calling. Mr. Kramer, of the yearling class, stepped inside.

"Mr. Spurlock requests me to inform Mr. Prescott that he demands a fight, at as early a moment as possible."

"My compliments to Mr. Spurlock, and I will meet him - here in barracks, to-night, I hope. Mr. Holmes has consented to act as one of my seconds."

"Very good, sir," nodded Yearling Kramer stiffly. "Mr. Holmes, will you step out and discuss the matter with me now?"

"Yes, sir," responded Greg. He was gone ten minutes. When he returned Greg announced:

"There's an extra room on the top floor of the next subdivision. The fight will take place there at nine to-night. Mr. Anstey has agreed to help look after your interests."

"All right, and thank you, old fellow," nodded Dick, as he turned to pick up a book.

Greg gulped and quivered behind his chum's back.

"He doesn't seem excited, but I know that I am," muttered Cadet Holmes. "The dear old fellow won't lose anything through nervousness, anyway."

Dick went through his studies and recitations as usual that day. If the stiff ordeal of the coming night carried any twinges for him, it wasn't noticeable in his demeanor. Yet Dick knew that the news had gotten thoroughly about among the cadets. He saw many of the new plebes gazing at him wonderingly.

When they returned from supper that night and reached their room, Greg was manifestly nervous - nervous enough for the pair of them, in fact.

"Dick, do you - do you expect to win?" asked Greg at last.

"Against a man like Mr. Spurlock?" smiled Cadet Prescott, and turned back to his study.

At a little after half past eight Mr. Anstey knocked on the door and came in.

"How's your form, Prescott, old ramrod?" the Virginian demanded.

"Fine, I hope," replied Dick laconically.

Greg heaved an inward sigh.

"Poor old Dick," he told himself. "I hate to see him hammered black and blue in a bare-knuckles fight like this one!"

CHAPTER IX

PLEBE PRESCOTT'S FIRST FIGHT

"We'd better get on hand early," advised Greg. "You want to take plenty of time about stripping for the fight. It would be throwing some of your chances away, Dick, for you to strip and prepare hurriedly, and step into the ring all flustered."

"You think I'm going to lose, don't you, Greg?" demanded Prescott grimly.

"Oh, I hope not," protested Cadet Holmes staunchly.

"But you think so, just the same," smiled Dick. "Now, Greg, do you remember the old Gridley High School spirit? Do you remember that our coaches told us to enter every battle on gridiron or diamond with the firm conviction that we couldn't be beaten? That's the old Grid. spirit that has been stealing over me the last few hours."

"It's a mighty good spirit to take into a fight," nodded Anstey.

Yet he, too, felt grave doubts that Prescott could come out of the approaching fight anything but a mass of pounded pulp. Mr. Spurlock was one of the highly accredited fighters of the yearling class.

"Well, we'd better be moving," nodded Greg. When they reached the unused room on the top floor of the next subdivision of plebes, they found Cadet Lieutenant Edwards and Mr. Jennison, both of the first class, already on hand. Mr. Devine, of the yearling class, who was to be one of Spurlock's seconds, was also in the room. There were two buckets of water, with sponges, and a supply of rough towels.

Almost immediately after Mr. Spurlock and Mr. Kramer came in.

Both of the principals now began to strip. Each had chosen the same fighting costume, consisting of old gray flannel trousers, belt,
rubber soled shoes and sleeveless sweater.

As Spurlock stood forth, arrayed for the battle, it was seen that he was a man of magnificent build for one of his years. His chest expansion was splendid. Over his chest and between his shoulders formidable muscles stood well out. His arms were not fat, but rather bulky with muscles. He made one think of a blacksmith.

Dick Prescott, being much lighter, did not make such an imposing appearance. Yet he did not strip to look like a weakling. His chest was fine, the muscles between his shoulder blades stood up well, while his arms, far smaller than Spurlock's, displayed the long, well-knit muscles of the Indian.

Two first class men had volunteered to act as the officials of the fight, since, in a cadet fight, none of the officials can ever be of the class represented by either combatant.

"Are you ready, gentlemen?" inquired Mr. Edwards, while Mr. Jennison drew out a watch that had served at many a cadet fight.

"Ready, sir," replied Spurlock. "Ready, sir," added Prescott. "This fight," announced the referee, "is to be to a finish. The rounds will last two minutes each, with a minute's rest between. Queensbury rules will be followed as far as they can be made to apply. This being a bare-knuckle fight for a matter of principle, the combatants will not shake hands."

There was an impressive pause, the referee turning to look at each fighter in turn.

Spurlock stood at ease, his arms folded over his chest, a grin on his face.

Plebe Prescott looked less confident. He stood with his fists clenched at his sides.

"Time!" called Mr. Edwards.

Spurlock unfolded his arms, throwing them in an attitude of semi-defense, as he coolly looked his opponent over.

Dick Prescott, on the other hand, threw his left foot forward, planting it firmly though lightly. His left arm raked outward, while his right fist came to a guard over his heart region.

"I suppose I've got to start this, as well as end it," jeered Mr. Spurlock. He made a sudden leap forward, throwing his offense low. Dick's left shot out to counter. Then Spurlock drove in, but Prescott got away by nimble dodging. Each man had now turned; the seconds jumped nimbly around, the referee following, while Jennison, his gaze mostly on the watch, jumped nimbly into a corner that he judged would not be used by the fighters.

"This isn't a sprint," sneered Spurlock, as he followed nimble Plebe Prescott around, Dick doing some saving dodging, ducking and sidestepping.

Nearly a dozen of Spurlock's blows Prescott succeeded in escaping, though the plebe was kept so busily on the defensive that he could not get back with anything to count.

"Stand up, you jumping-jack!" hissed Spurlock.

He did get in a short-arm jab on Dick's right lower ribs that made the plebe gasp audibly.

Spurlock now started in to take advantage of this by getting the plebe going. Dick, however, dodged less and countered better. He took two nasty blows, then Mr. Jennison called.

"Time!"

"You're standing him off a heap better than I thought you could," whispered Anstey, as he and Greg sponged the plebe fighter off quickly and then began to knead his muscles. While this was still going on the referee again summoned the fighters forward.

The second round started. As before, Prescott kept mainly on the defensive, though always watching his chance to come back at his more powerful opponent. Spurlock began to press his man hard, when, of a sudden, Prescott got in low under the other's guard, came up and landed a blow on the Spurlock nose that brought the first blood of the fight.

With an angry growl Spurlock leaped in now, to chase and wind up his younger opponent.

But Dick did some nimble dodging, devoting his attention largely to defending his eyes from assault.

Then, in turning, suddenly, Dick let one leg drag an instant behind him. Spurlock, following like lightning, aimed a blow, but it fell short, for he tripped over Dick's leg and fell sprawling.

Referee, time-keeper and plebe principals laughed. Spurlock's seconds scowled.

But Dick generously drew back five or six feet, standing on the defensive until Mr. Spurlock leaped to his feet, ready to renew the combat.

Spurlock, however, had hurt one of his knees, in going down, just enough to interfere with his nimbleness of pursuit during the rest of the round. Time-keep Jennison soon ended that round.

"Mister," growled Yearling Kramer, turning around while Dick sat between his seconds being sponged and kneaded, "don't be so much of a coward! Don't run away and delay the finish. Stand up as if you had some manhood!"

"Thank you, sir," replied Dick coldly. "I'm managing my end of this fight."

"You b.j. little poltroon," snarled Kramer. "I'll call you out myself if you have the nerve to talk back!" hissed Kramer.

"Is licking cowards your specialty?" demanded Prescott coolly.

But that settled it, making a coming fight with Kramer an absolute necessity, now.

"Mr. Kramer," interrupted Mr. Edwards sternly, "this has gone far enough. You must stop hectoring that plebe, sir. He has all he can attend to as it is."

Kramer stopped, with a snap of the jaws. He didn't want to. But a hint, on a matter of etiquette, or the code, from the first class man, was as valid as a command. And Mr. Edwards had spoken in a tone that was authoritative enough.

"You run all you want," whispered Greg indignantly. "You have a right to. This room is smaller than a Queensbury ring."

"I shan't stop my footwork unless the referee orders it," replied Prescott, in an under-tone.

"You're doing just right," nodded Anstey. "If you weren't Mr. Edwards would stop it. He's running this fight on the fair-and-square. If I have a fight I hope it will be my luck to have Mr.

Edwards running the job."

"How do you feel?" asked Anstey, in an undertone.

"All right," returned Dick. "But I had to trust to footwork to save myself. Mr. Spurlock got nearly all my wind in that other round."

"Is your wind in again?" asked Greg anxiously.

"Yes; I think I feel as fine as my man does," replied Dick, stepping up from the care of his handlers to await the command.

"Isn't Mr. Kramer the brute?" whispered Anstey indignantly.

"I'm not going to think of him, now," answered Plebe Prescott over his shoulder. "I have all I can attend to at present."

"I'll get him now, Kramer," muttered Spurlock, as he rose. "Watch me reduce that b.j. plebe to powder! I hope they have a spare cot for him over at hospital."

Again the referee set them at it.

Mr. Spurlock encountered a mild surprise, for now Dick seemed less inclined to trust to his nimble feet. He put up a stand-up front, though several of Spurlock's sledge-hammer blows passed over Dick's falling head.

Then the yearling began to fight lower.

The plebe put up a good series of counters, though he took another bit of punishment in the short ribs, and began to back away.

Across the room, Mr. Spurlock began driving his victim, slowly but systematically.

H. Irving Hancock

Dick retreated, putting up the best guard he could, dodging when he had to.

But the yearling, full of the grim spirit of the thing, pursued without undue haste, driving the plebe, a foot at a time, clean across the room toward the opposite wall.

At last Spurlock had his victim all but leaning against the wall, sorely pressed. Then, with a sudden tensing of his muscles, the yearling let his left drive to "paste" the plebe's head against the hard wall.

CHAPTER X

THE "BEAST" WHO SCORED

SMASH!

But the plebe wasn't there. Dick Prescott had counted on this, and had wriggled out by a duck and a plunge forward that carried him beyond momentary risk of Mr. Spurlock's following right.

The yearling's left fist landed with such force as to cause a half square yard of plaster to fall with a thud.

With a yell of disgust Spurlock wheeled about, but the plebe was waiting for him.

At just the right instant, Dick let fly with all his might with his own left.

It caught the yearling over the right eye, closing it.

Just three or four feet back danced Prescott, then came forward again. A blow set the yearling's nose to bleeding afresh.

Then bang! went the other eye closed. The upper class men gasped with astonishment, for Spurlock was now getting into bad shape.

He was all but dazed, in fact; and had twenty-five seconds yet

H. Irving Hancock

to go in the round.

Then, as much in mercy as for anything else, Dick Prescott dropped his left against the yearling's jawbone.

There was a crash as the dazed man went to the floor.

Instantly Mr. Jennison's voice rose, counting:

"One, two, three, four -"

"Take the full count, Spurdy," advised Kramer, bending forward over his principal.

"- eight, nine, ten!" gasped out the timekeeper.

Mr. Spurlock had shown no sign of rising. In fact, he was still unconscious.

"I award the fight to Mr. Prescott," called the cool, exact tones of Mr. Edward.

Greg could have let out a whoop and danced a war-dance, but in the presence of upper class men this plebe had to restrain himself. Anstey's eyes flashed, but otherwise the Virginian bore himself modestly.

"Carry Mr. Spurlock down to the door. Then summon stretcher-bearers from the hospital," directed Mr. Edwards.

It was Yearling Devine who sprang to obey this direction.

Now Dick spoke, ever so quietly.

"Mr. Kramer, I understood that you did me the honor to call me out."

"Eh?" muttered that other yearling. "Oh, yes; so I did. Whenever you're ready, mister!"

"If Mr. Edwards and Mr. Jennison are willing," returned the plebe coolly, "I'm ready as soon as Mr. Spurlock has been carried away."

"Oho, mister! B.j. to the end, are you?"

"No, sir; only anxious to atone for my b.j.-ety," replied Cadet Prescott, with a little flash of his eyes.

Anstey had gone below with Devine, to render any help that could be given.

"This is rather unusual, mister," suggested Mr. Edwards, glancing at his watch. "However, if you really feel fit, and if it suits Mr. Kramer -"

"Oh, anything will suit me," returned the yearling. Truth to tell, Kramer wasn't by any means sure that he could whip this crafty plebe. But the issue had been thrown fairly in his teeth. Moreover, the honor of the yearling class was now at stake, and Kramer wasn't the man to go back on his class.

"Listen, gentlemen," broke in Mr. Edwards. "This affair started a little ahead of the time set. It is now nine-fifteen. In ten minutes or less, we can have Mr. Spurlock on his way to cadet hospital. Then, if you two mix it up spicily, we can have the affair over by nine-forty. In any case I shall have to call the fight by that time, and decide it a draw, if necessary. What say you?"

"Quite satisfactory, sir," nodded Kramer.

"Satisfactory, sir," added Prescott, waiting, as a plebe should, until the yearling had spoken.

Devine was back almost at once. The seconds carried the still unconscious Mr. Spurlock below to the waiting stretcher. Immediately after Kramer dropped in on a classmate, who gladly came upstairs to aid Mr. Devine in seconding

Mr. Kramer.

Not an unnecessary moment did Mr. Kramer lose with his stripping. He was ready in almost record time, presenting, bared, a man of about Mr. Spurlock's proportions, weight and general muscular fitness.

Mr. Edwards quickly recited the conditions, then called for the start of the affair.

Figuring that Prescott must now be a good deal sore and at least a bit winded, Mr. Kramer started in at a lively gait, trying to bear the plebe down with swift, overpowering rushes and showers of blows.

Some of these landed on the plebe's sturdy body, the whacks resounding. But the blows merely stirred Prescott's fighting blood within him. Standing up fairly, with little footwork, but displaying much more speed, Dick Prescott drove in blow after blow in such bewildering succession as to all but daze the yearling.

Bang! Kramer's right eye was half closed just as Cadet Jennison called the end of the first round.

"Great Scott, but that little fellow is a canned hurricane!" muttered Devine, as he wrung out cloths in cold water and applied then to Kramer's swelling eye. "Old man, you want to swing one blow down on the top of his head, and crush him, if you want to save your personal appearance."

"Won't I?" grunted Kramer. "Just watch me. I won't murder the plebe, but I've stood all the fooling I'm going to."

As the combatants rushed at each other again Kramer struck out two or three times; then clinched to save himself.

"Break away, there!" admonished Edwards sternly. "Get off!"

Again in that round Kramer clinched, despite the referee's sternest orders.

"That's no way to meet a plebe, Mr. Kramer," cried Edwards disgustedly.

After the second get-away Dick fairly danced around his man. A blow on the nose brought Kramer's blood. Then his left eye went all but shut. At that the yearling spun dizzily. Dick drove a light blow in behind his man's ear. Down went Spurlock's "avenger" sprawling on the floor.

Mr. Jennison began to count while Kramer lay on the floor, stirring uneasily, yet not seeming to comprehend his seconds' warnings.

"- eight, nine, ten!" finished Mr. Jennison, then put the watch in his pocket.

"The fight is awarded to Mr. Prescott, and it isn't nine thirty yet," announced Mr. Edwards.

Dick's jubilant seconds sponged him, rubbed him down, kneaded his muscles and joyously assisted him in dressing.

Kramer, coming to presently, but with a face that Anstey said "made him think of the Dismal Swamp," was assisted downstairs by his seconds, and taken to the cadet hospital.

With the exception of the two yearlings whom Cadet Prescott had thrashed to a finish, all who had taken any part in the fights were in their beds, and lights out, when the subdivision inspectors flashed their bull's-eye lanterns into the room a moment after taps had sounded.

For the honor of the class another yearling, Garston, forced a dispute within a few days, and Prescott had his third fight on his hands. He won it, though, about as easily as he had the other two.

Three such victories left this plebe free from further fight annoyance. Also, according to a tacitly understood rule, none of these three yearlings could engage in hazing Mr. Prescott after that.

CHAPTER XI

HOW CADET DODGE HELD POST NUMBER THREE

In the early days of the month of June, came all the glories of Commencement.

The first class graduated, and went forth to receive their commissions in the Regular Army.

The second class became the new first class, and head and arbiters of all personal affairs in the battalion of cadets.

The yearlings now became second class men, and departed on their summer furlough, to last until the latter part of August.

The old plebes moved up a peg, also, and became the new yearlings, vested with all the power of hazing and otherwise oppressing and training the plebes.

But for the new plebes - what? They were plebes just as much as ever, and would be until the following June.

The day after the graduating class had departed, and the late yearlings had followed in their trail, as the furloughed new second class, what was left of the battalion marched forth out of barracks into camp.

Here under the khaki-colored tents what was left of the battalion settled down to the life of the soldier in the field.

H. Irving Hancock

An untrained eye might not have noticed much in the arrangement of the camp. However, the tents of the main camp were arranged along six company streets. There was also the larger tent of the tactical officer in charge, the guard-tent, and some other tents used in the administration of camp-life.

Now, every text-book was laid aside for the summer. Instruction during camp period was to be in the practical duties that belong to the soldier's life.

The new first class mourned the loss of a few members who had been "found" - that is, who had failed in their studies just before Commencement. More than a score had been dropped from the new yearling class. Only two of the new plebes had been dropped, they having been found wholly and absolutely unfit to keep the brain-fagging pace of academic work at West Point.

"I never minded study back home," muttered Greg, as he and Dick toiled setting their few belongings to rights under canvas. "But, the way the study-gait is kept up here at West Point, I certainly say 'hurrah' with all my heart at the thought that books are closed for all summer."

"We'll be back at the grind in September again," laughed Dick. "And I'm assured that we haven't struck the real study-gait yet; that these new three months from March on are only to break us in a bit, so that we won't mind the real thing so much when we meet it in September."

"Then you give me cause for gloomy thought," shuddered Greg.

"Make way for a future general," grinned Anstey, as, with both arms full of belongings he forced his way into the tent. The cadets were housed three to a tent, and Anstey, to the great delight of Dick and Greg, had been assigned to bunk with them. Anstey, too, was delighted, for the young Virginian was a gentleman of the actual type, who had been growing steadily more weary of the sham "gentleman" that Bert Dodge had so far illustrated.

"I'm tent orderly this week," announced Dick, with a grin. "I received that very important news five minutes ago. I'm responsible for the order and condition of the tent for this week, so you fellows will have to step around to keep the tent in style to suit me."

"Oh, if you're tent orderly," laughed Anstey, "then we don't have to take the word from you."

"You don't?" demanded Prescott.

"No, indeed. If you're the orderly, then you're merely a striker."

A "striker," in the Army, is an enlisted man who is paid by an officer for doing servant's work in spare time. Hence, a striker is, in general, anyone engaged in menial service.

"Come on, Holmesy," urged Anstey, rising. "We'll go out for a stroll. Striker, see to it that you have a flawless tent interior when we return."

In his glee Anstey seized Greg by one arm and started to rush him out of the tent.

"Oh, all right; go along," gibed Dick. "See who'll get the lash though, when I turn in my report."

"Would you skin us?" demanded Anstey, halting in the doorway of the tent and gazing back with a look of mock horror.

To "skin" a brother cadet is to report him for some dereliction in duty, thereby bringing down discipline upon the offender.

"Skin you?" repeated Dick. "Yes, sir! If you leave me to bring order out of all this military chaos I'll hand you in to the O.C.

in a way that will take every square inch of cuticle from your body."

"Traitor!" hissed Anstey tragically.

"Mister, it's a whole year yet before plebes can sing, laugh, or be happy," came the muttered warning, as one of the newly-made yearlings passed by the tent.

Anstey became silent at once. He had been at West Point long enough to know his place as a plebe.

"Say," whispered Anstey presently, his eyes brimming over with glee, "have you seen poor old Dodge to-day?"

"Not particularly," responded Prescott.

"Well, he's the maddest rookie (recruit) you ever saw! Having been old Dodge's roommate up to reveille this morning, I am in a position to state that he took advantage of the general laxity last night, and slipped out of barracks after taps last night. He and some other embryo cadets got a rowboat, through connivance with a soldier in the engineer's detachment. They rowed across the river, to Garrison, and had some kind of high old racket. It must have been high," added Anstey pensively, "for I happened to turn over in bed this morning, and I saw old Dodge slipping back into the room about an hour before reveille."

"Well, what's he mad about, now?" demanded Dick.

"Why, he has been drawn for the new guard! He's on guard for to-day and to-night!" chuckled Anstey gleefully. "Already dead for sleep, his official duties will keep him without much more sleep for twenty-four hours, or until the new guard goes on to-morrow. Even then he'll have some other things to take up some of his time."

By-and-by the tent was so much and well to rights that, when

Cadet Corporal Brodie, of the new yearling class, looked in, he could find no fault with its appearance.

Dick sat down on his box. Greg did the same. Plebes are not allowed campstools in the summer encampment - probably on the theory that so much luxury would be certain to demoralize them.

"I'm going out for a wee bit stroll," drawled Anstey, after taking a look in the tiny soldier's mirror to see that his appearance was in apple-pie order.

"Don't make the mistake of forgetting, and calling on one of the new yearlings," cautioned Dick dryly.

"There's no trace of insanity in our family history," responded Anstey gravely, as he stepped outside.

Dick and Greg found they had much to talk about in comparing notes of what each had learned about the nature of duties in the summer camp. They were still thus engaged when Anstey bounded back into the tent. The young Virginian looked as though he were having a tremendously hard time to keep himself from exploding.

"Oh, this is rich!" he chuckled.

"What is?" inquired Dick, looking up in some mystification.

"What do you suppose Dodge has gone and done, now?"

"Said a kind word about me?" smiled Prescott.

"I didn't say anything about miracles," drawled the Virginian. "No; poor old Dodge has drawn number three post for guard duty on the late tour to-night!"

"Well, isn't three a good enough number?" asked Greg innocently.

H. Irving Hancock

"A good post, you meandering old puddin'-head!" retorted Anstey. "Good? The post that goes by old Fort Clinton?"

"Well, it is a bit lonely, off there in the woods," admitted Cadet Prescott.

"Lonely?" bubbled over Anstey. "And you've seen the ditch that runs along by that post?"

"Naturally," nodded Dick. "You will probably remember that I got past the eye-sight tests of the rainmakers" (doctors).

"Now, I've just been talking with a young cit. fellow, who's visiting one of the officers on post," continued Anstey. "He tells me that, every year, some of the yearlings slyly waylay a plebe whenever they can catch him pacing on number three post late at night."

"What do they do to him?" questioned Prescott.

"Oh, they don't do a thing to him, I reckon," drawled the Virginian. "At least, nothing that a jovial fellow can object to. They may roll him down in the ditch, take his gun away from him, and hide it, or some little thing like that."

"Then, see here," proposed Dick solemnly, "Dodge may not be the most popular fellow in the corps, but he's one of us, anyway. He belongs to our class. Anything that is done against him is, in a measure, done to the whole class. Anstey, we ought to get Dodge aside and warn him."

"Warn him?" repeated Anstey aghast. "Warn him - and spoil all the fun!"

"I know I'd want to be warned, if it were likely to happen to me to-night," insisted Dick soberly.

"Oh - well, I don't know but that you're right," assented Anstey slowly. "Yes; I'm certain you are."

"Hullo, you raw-looking rookies," hailed Dodge, halting and looking in through the doorway.

"Come in here a minute, Dodge," urged Anstey.

For an instant Dodge looked suspicious. Then he muttered:

"As you're not yearlings, I accept the invitation."

Very spick and span Dodge looked as he entered the tent. As a member of the guard he wore a pair of immaculate white duck trousers, which held the "spooniest" crease imaginable. His gray coat and white gloves made him look more the dandy than usual.

"We've something to tell you, Dodge," Anstey continued almost in a whisper, as the four plebes stood in a close bunch. "At least, old ramrod says we ought to tell you."

Then, lowering his voice still more, Anstey gave an outline of what the new yearlings were supposed to try to do to the lonely plebe on post number three at the hour when ghosts walk.

"Humph!" rejoined Dodge quickly. "Let the yearlings try that sort of trick, if they dare. Have those fellows no idea of the sacred position of trust held by a United States sentinel? For I, on sentry duty, represent the sovereignty of the United States just as much as does any soldier patrolling a lonely post in the face of the enemy in war time!"

"All very well," grinned Dick "But how are you going to prove it, if the yearlings catch you napping tonight?"

"They won't," retorted Dodge pompously. "They shan't. And if any fellow, I don't care who he is, tries to rush my post to-night he'll feel the steel of one of Uncle Sam's bayonets prodding him in the tenderest part of his worthless carcass!"

"Look out, Dodge!" cautioned Greg softly. "Don't let any of

the yearlings hear you canning a brag like that, or they'll get you if they have to turn out the whole class after taps to do the job."

"Let 'em try it!" insisted Dodge. "And you fellows are at liberty to tell anyone that I said it."

With that the speaker turned and strolled out of the tent, looking rather miffed.

"The pompous old idiot!" muttered Anstey, in a tone of pained disgust. "Oh, why did ever fond parents let a mentally irresponsible chap like that come to a place like West Point for anyway?"

"Our skirts are clear, anyway," remarked Dick Prescott consolingly. "We told him all we knew. If he doesn't act upon it, it's his rifle, not ours, that gets fouled."

Dodge not only believed the hoax to be impossible, with him on number three, but he was incautious enough to talk about it freely among the plebes during the day.

As was almost certain to happen, one of the yearlings heard Dodge sounding his trumpet of brag. That yearling, on the other side of a tent wall, grinned, and presently took counsel with other yearlings.

It was almost at the stroke of taps that night when Bert Dodge marched from guard tent with the relief under Cadet Corporal Hasbrouck.

As the other sentry on number three fell in, and Dodge stepped out to take up his vigil, Corporal Hasbrouck gave added instructions to the new and untried sentry.

"Sometimes, Mr. Dodge, this post has been known to be about as dangerous as one in war time."

"Yes, sir, answered Dodge respectfully, as he was bound to. Then as the cadet corporal marched on with the relief, Dodge glanced after the vanishing squad to mutter to himself:

"What a lot of nonsense. I'd like to see anyone rush me!"

"I wonder what Dodge will do on number three to-night," yawned Anstey, just before the three tentmates fell asleep.

"Oh, I wonder what it will be," grinned Greg.

Then the three went sound asleep.

Dick turned later and awoke just in time to hear the voice of a sentry calling:

"Half past eleven! Post number one, and all's we-ell!"

Then, a little further away, another voice took up the refrain:

"Post num-ber two, and all's we-ell!"

"Jupiter!" gasped sleepy Prescott, becoming instantly wide awake. "Post number three doesn't answer. They've gone and got old Dodge."

There was a rapid sound of feet in the company street as Corporal Hasbrouck and the guard rushed along at double quick.

"Hey, you - wake up!" commanded Dick, vigorously prodding the plebe sleepers on either side of him.

"All present, sir!" sleepily mumbled Anstey.

"What's up?" demanded Greg, sitting up.

"The very deuce!" retorted Dick. "There! Listen to that!"

"Bang!" sounded a rifle report. Then Corporal Hasbrouck's bellowing voice could be heard:

"Officer of the day, post number three!" Some one could be heard running down the street. A few moments passed, during which Dick, Greg and Anstey sat up on their mattresses listening eagerly.

Then came the officer of the day running back.

There was another brief pause, or just long enough for the officer of the day to make a report to the O.C. and to receive orders.

Tr-r-rat-tat-tat-tat! The drummers at guard tent were running out the crisp summons of assembly.

"Get up! Tumble out lively for general roll call!" muttered Dick, springing to his feet.

"What in the mischief can they have done to old Dodge?" wondered Greg as he hurriedly pulled on his shoes.

"You men will turn out instantly," ordered a cadet corporal, thrusting his head in at the tent doorway. "Elaborate dressing isn't necessary."

Dick bolted out, followed by Anstey, Greg bringing up the ear.

Cadets by scores and hundreds were falling in by companies, while the company commanders stood by watchful and alert.

Only the members of the guard were excused from this assembly.

Almost instantly orders rang out crisply, and the ranks closed. Then the cadet adjutant, the roll in his hands, began to call the names by companies, holding a pencil in readiness to check down any cadet found absent.

Back of the adjutant stood the cadet officer of the day and Captain Vesey, of the Army, who was the tac. doing duty as O.C.

The calling of the roll, while the cadets stood in ranks, wondering, brought a surprise to Captain Vesey. Every cadet supposed to be in camp was present or satisfactorily accounted for.

"When dismissed," rang the cadet adjutant's voice, "men not on duty will return to their tents and finish the night's rest. Dismiss by companies."

As the drowsy cadets turned back to their company streets there was a buzz of eager, under-toned conversation. Some of the men of the guard threw in enough information so that the main part of the story became known and flew like fire through the camp.

When post number three failed to answer at half past eleven Corporal Hasbrouck and a squad of the guard went to that post in double-quick time.

Dodge was found to be absent from his post, but his rifle, with bayonet fixed, was securely tied to a near-by bush in the position of "port arms."

Dodge simply was not to be found. At one point signs of a scuffle had been found, but the trail, after starting down the slope, soon disappeared.

Cadet Dodge could not be found. No one, unless some unidentified hazers, knew where that young sentry was.

Assembly had been sounded and all cadets called out for roll call in order that it might be learned what cadets, if any, were absent from camp without authority. But roll each had failed to show any absentees.

Captain Vesey was furious. So was Lieutenant-Colonel Strong, the commandant of cadets, who had just been summoned, and who was now at the tac. tent questioning Hasbrouck and others.

Through the night no trace was found of Mr. Dodge.

CHAPTER XII

PRESCOTT GETS NUMBER THREE

When the cadet battalion marched off to mess the following morning the mystery of Cadet Dodge's whereabouts was as big a mystery as ever.

At the tent of the O.C., however, things were seething. As soon as the battalion returned to camp cadets were sent for in rapid succession.

However, the trail remained as blind as ever. The various detachments were ordered out for drill or practical instruction.

Our three young cadets were marched nearly two miles for instruction in target practice. At the outset this work was with the gallery rifle at short ranges.

At the close of practice the squad was marched back over the dusty roads.

"Dodge has been found," was the smiling word passed around as this detachment of plebes was dismissed inside camp limits.

"Where? How? When?"

The amazing story was told with a good deal of quiet laughter.

At about half past eight this morning one of the workmen

106   H. Irving Hancock

employed in a lumber yard at Garrison, across the river, walking in behind a pile of lumber close to the river, was amazed to find a pillow slip lying on the ground. What was much more astonishing was the fact that a waist and a pair of legs protruded from the pillowcase, and the feet were bound.

The workman, a dull-witted fellow, thought he had stumbled upon a case of murder, and rushed back to the office. The manager thereupon hurried to the spot and the mystery was quickly solved.

The pillowcase being removed, they saw Mr. Dodge, bound and gagged.

He was promptly set free and questioned. But he refused any information to the manager of the lumber yard, beyond stating that he had been the victim of an outrage.

On the next trip of the ferry across the river Mr. Dodge returned, the lumber yard manager accompanying him. Mr. Dodge had reported, with a very crestfallen air, at the guard tent, and from there had been hurried on to Captain Vesey's tent. Now the story came out.

Mr. Dodge had just given the eleven o'clock hail, the night before, when he was suddenly seized from behind and thrown flat. A pillowcase was slipped over his head while he was held by so many that struggling was out of the question. By the time the pillowcase had been pulled down over his head Mr. Dodge also discovered that he had been swiftly but most effectively bound.

For the rest he knew only that he had been carried down the slope, unable to give any alarm, and that he had been lifted into a boat, taken over the river and dumped in the lumber yard. Here he had spent the rest of the night and the early morning until found. He had tried, repeatedly, to free himself, but had failed.

This was all the material on which Captain Vesey, and his superior, Lieutenant-Colonel Strong, had upon which to work, save for Dodge's admission that he had been warned, the day before, by Cadets Prescott, Holmes and Anstey. These three were accordingly summoned to the O.C.'s tent and asked to explain.

"Mr. Prescott," asked Captain Vesey, "why did you warn Mr. Dodge? What information had you that such an outrage on a sentry was being planned?"

"I knew only what Mr. Anstey had told me, sir," replied Dick at once.

"Mr. Anstey," demanded Captain Vesey, turning to the Virginian, "what information did you have, and how did you obtain it?"

Back of the O.C. sat the K.C. (commandant of cadets), his dark eyes fixed upon the witnesses.

"All the information I had, sir, was what a young cit. with whom I talked yesterday morning told me about pranks that had been played in past years upon plebes who had the late tour of post number three."

"Your statement is that you had a conversation with a citizen, and that he told you of pranks that had been played in former years?"

"Yes, sir; that was the intent of my statement."

"The citizen with whom you talked did not give you any hint that a trick might be played last night?"

"No, sir; only in the general way that the citizen's stories made me half suspect that something might be tried last night."

"Because Mr. Dodge was a plebe?"

"Yes, sir.

"And also because the plebe was Mr. Dodge?" Anstey hesitated an instant, then shot out promptly.

"Yes, sir."

"Why did you think that Mr. Dodge was extremely likely to be singled out?"

Cadet Anstey flushed and again hesitated.

"You are not required to say anything distinctly to the discredit or disadvantage of Mr. Dodge, but you are required, Mr. Anstey, to give any information that will aid the authorities in running down this outrage and its perpetrators. Again, sir, why did you imagine that Mr. Dodge would be singled out?"

"I knew, sir, that a good many upper class men regarded Mr. Dodge as being decidedly b.j.," the Virginian admitted reluctantly.

"Then you attribute this affair to Mr. Dodge's unpopularity with some of the upper class men?"

"I wouldn't say, sir, that Mr. Dodge is unpopular, but I think, sir, that some of the upper class men feel that Mr. Dodge needs taking in hand."

"For hazing?"

"For - er - well, sir - for general training."

"That is hazing - nothing more nor less," broke in the K.C. coldly. "And we shall leave no stone unturned to stop this hazing and to punish all perpetrators of hazing."

"Did Mr. Dodge accept your warning?" continued Captain Vesey.

"He did not, sir."

"Mr. Anstey, on your word as a cadet and a gentleman, you have told me all you know of the affair?"

"Yes, sir."

"Mr. Prescott, on your word as a cadet and a gentleman, have you told me all you know?"

"Yes, sir," Dick replied. "That is, sir, all except what is common knowledge to all, yourself included, sir."

"Mr. Holmes, have you any knowledge bearing on this subject, in addition to what has been stated by these other cadets?"

"None, sir."

"That is all for the present," nodded Captain Vesey. "You may go."

As soon as the cadets were out of hearing the "tac." turned to the K.C.

"The motive back of this outrage on a sentry is all quite clear to me, Colonel," spoke the subordinate officer. "Dodge is an unpopular and b.j.-ish fellow. He has undoubtedly been making his brags that he'd bag any yearlings who tried to interfere with him on post. Some of the yearlings must have taken up the challenge."

"Yet at roll call last night, which was held at once, every cadet responded or was properly accounted for," broke in the K.C. savagely.

"Yes, Colonel; but the young men had nearly half an hour in which to work."

"They couldn't have rowed both ways across the Hudson and

have gotten back into camp in time for that swift roll call," retorted Colonel Strong.

"Even that part of the affair doesn't seem very puzzling to me, sir," replied Captain Vesey. "Assuming that yearlings bagged Mr. Dodge, as I think they did, they may have had citizen friends at hand to carry out the rest of the affair with a boat. They may even have arranged with soldiers belonging to one of the Army detachments here."

"The only matter of importance now, Captain Vesey, is to find out just which cadets, if cadets were engaged in the outrage, seized Mr. Dodge on his post."

"In ferreting them out, Colonel, I will follow to the last extremity any instructions you may give me, sir," promised Captain Vesey.

The K.C. tugged hard at his moustache, then scowled harder than before.

"What do you think the chances are, Vesey, of our finding the perpetrators?"

"Frankly, Colonel, I don't think we have a chance in a million, unless some yearling concerned in the matter voluntarily confesses."

"A yearling voluntarily confess!" snorted the K.C. rising. "Bah!"

Captain Vesey smiled after his superior officer had stalked out of the tent. It is just barely possible that the younger officer, remembering some prank of his own yearling days, wasn't extraordinarily anxious to detect yearlings in an offense that would result in depriving the Army of the further services of some very bright and resourceful young men.

Hot, dusty, perspiring, first class men, yearlings and plebes came back to camp in detachments from various tours of drum and instruction. The only cadets who looked at all fresh were the members of the guard, who were excused from the day's drills. Yet for these returning ones, late in the afternoon of a hot day, there was no immediate rest. Some of the cadets came back in service clothes, others in khaki, still others in field costume of campaign hat, flannel shirt, gray trousers and leggins. Immediately the young men in all these varieties of uniform disappeared within their tents. There was a subdued sound of great bustle. Then, almost in the same instant, it seemed, cadets stepped from the various tents into the open. Each was immaculate, very nearly glorious in spotless, faultlessly pressed white duck trousers, topped by the gray full-dress coat and hat. Each cadet carried his rifle now, except for the cadet officers, who wore their swords.

With almost dizzying speed, after the return and the dressing, the assembly was sounded. The company to which Dick and his mates belonged was then, at the command, formed and inspected, marched across the plain, over to the parade ground, where hundreds of girls, in bright-hued dresses, and other visitors to West Point awaited their coming.

With the cadet adjutant and cadet sergeant-major in place as guides, the company came to its place in battalion formation. Other companies marched in, and parade rest was ordered. Now, at the command, a few movements in the manual of arms were executed, the battalion presenting a beautiful line of gray, white and flashing steel. Next the band, playing gayly, marched from left of line, before the battalion, halting in place beyond the right of line. Fifes and drums sounded the retreat. The sunset gun boomed over the hollow beyond; down came the Stars and Stripes on one more day of national life, while the band played "The Star Spangled Banner" and all the men and boys among the spectators, including several on-looking Army officers, uncovered their heads, standing rigidly at attention. It was an awe-inspiring moment to one who could feel the thrill of patriotism. This whole ceremony of dress parade had about it the impressive solemnity of religious worship.

There were yet some more formalities. Then the young men were marched back. A few minutes after the sunset gun the men were once more in their own company streets, and, for all cadets except those of the guard, the work day was over. In the evening there was to be a cadet hop at Cullom Hall, at which many of the bright-faced girls who had watched dress parade would be present. The evening after there would be a band concert in camp. So the nights of the cadet summer were passed.

But the hops were not for the plebes. They could dance only in the day time, under the watchful eyes of the dancing instructor, for every plebe must take dancing lessons in summer until he has been pronounced qualified. To a cadet hop, though there is no official rule against it, no plebe ever presumes to go. Nor may he, for that matter, mingle in the social life with the young lady visitors at the post. He may try it, of course, but no well-informed girl will allow a plebe to take the chances. If a plebe is caught actually paying attention to any young woman the upper class men take care of him in their own effective way. A plebe, like any other cadet, must show courtesy to any woman who addresses him; beyond that the young man must not go during his plebedom. "Flirtation Week" is close by, but no plebe ever dares to stroll there.

This being the night of the hop, the upper class men were busy with their toilets as soon as they returned from supper; or as many of them were as had arranged to "drag a femme" to the hop. This is cadet parlance for escorting a young lady to the dance. However, some upper class men notoriously avoid attending hops.

"It's a fine thing, isn't it," growled Greg that evening, "to take a lot of dancing lessons every week, and then, when the night comes around, to stroll through the company streets and listen to the orchestra in the distance."

"I'm not complaining," Dick replied.

"Yet you used to be fond of dancing."

"I am now."

"Then why don't you yearn to go to a hop?"

"I do. But see here, Greg. The fellow makes the best soldier, in the end, I'll wager, who learns to keep his greatest desires in check. All the restrictions thrown around the plebe by custom are intended to make him the better man, soldier and officer by teaching him to wait until his time comes."

"I congratulate you, mister," spoke a low but hearty voice from the doorway of a tent the two plebes were passing. "You're coming on, mister. Grin and bear it. You'll be happy one of these days!"

Dick and Greg glanced backward over their shoulders to see that the speaker was Mr. Reynolds, member of the new first class and a cadet captain. Reynolds usually attended the hops. But for to-night he had only a telegram in the breast of his coat in the place of the cherished "femme" whom he had hoped to "drag." As he stood in his doorway, looking up at the inscrutable stars, Cadet Captain Reynolds was taking his own lesson in patient waiting.

"Thank you, sir," Dick replied in a low tone, then faced front again.

That night another plebe was on post number three during the tour ending at midnight. He was not molested, however, which was most fortunate for mischief-loving yearlings, for the K.C. had stationed two tacs. in hiding close by, to be promptly on hand in case of any attempted trouble.

A few nights later it came Dick Prescott's turn to take the late tour on post number three. He was both apprehensive and watchful, but when the relief picked him up at midnight he had no report of any kind to make.

It was well enough known throughout cadet camp that the superintendent and all his subordinates were bent sternly on stopping or severely punishing any attempts to interfere with sentries.

As the weeks of hard work passed, and no more mysteries fell over post number three it began to be felt that plebes might thereafter walk there on the darkest night without worry.

One day in July Dick found himself again on guard, with post number three for the "ghosts promenade" - that is, the tour ending at midnight.

"Don't feel too secure, will you, old man?" begged Anstey. "Watch out, just the same, won't you?"

"I always take that post as though it were one of especial danger," Dick answered seriously.

Which was well indeed, for Yearlings Davis, Graham and Poultney were even then plotting behind the walls of their tent.

CHAPTER XIII

THE SENTRY MAKES A CAPTURE

"Post number one! Eleven o'clock, and all's well."

"Post number two! Eleven o'clock, and all's well!"

Cadet Prescott, midway on his post, came to a halt, bringing his rifle to port arms.

"Post number three! Eleven o'clock, and all's well."

Nor did the plebe return his rifle to his shoulder and resume pacing until he heard the hail taken up and repeated by the man on number four. Thus the call traveled the rounds, back to number one, and died out.

Just an instant later Plebe Prescott became suspicious that something was wrong in his immediate vicinity.

Rain was threatening, and the sultry night was so dark that, on this shaded post, the young sentry could see barely a few yards away from him.

Yet Dick was certain he saw something flash darkly by, not far away. It could hardly have been a shadow. Whatever it was, a clump of bushes now concealed the moving something.

"Halt! Who's there?" hailed Cadet Prescott. He stopped to

listen, bringing his rifle once more down to port arms.

There was no response.

Certain, however, that his senses had not been deluded, the young sentry stepped quickly toward the clump of bushes.

From the other side of the bushes came a sudden sound of scrambling.

"Halt! Who's there?" demanded Prescott again.

Whoever it was, and plainly there was more than one man there, the prowlers had no mind to be held up by the sentry or the guard.

"Halt, or I'll run a bayonet into you!" shouted Prescott resolutely. "Corporal of the guard, post number three!" he bellowed aloud.

At the same time he was darting after the fugitives, whom it was too dark to distinguish. From the very little that his eyes could make out, however, it was his belief that the running men were cadets.

Then one must have stumbled and fallen, for a figure lay between two bushes as Prescott dashed up.

"Don't you attempt to rise until you get the word, or you'll feel the jab of my bayonet," warned Dick.

He couldn't follow the others much further, anyway, as he had no authority to leave his post. The man on number four must have heard, and would be alert.

"Where are you, number three sentry!" came Cadet Corporal Brodie's hail.

"Here, sir!" Dick answered. He still stood watching the figure that lay in the shadow of the bushes. The fallen one had not attempted to move. Dick Prescott was close enough to make a thrust with his bayonet-tipped rifle if the fallen one made any effort to leap up.

That was as close as Dick intended to get until help was at hand, for an old trick with cadets running the guard on a dark night on this lonely stretch was to wait until the sentry got close enough, then to reach out and grab him by the ankles, throwing him.

Always, when such a trick was played successfully, the offender would be up, off and safe by the time the thrown sentry was on his own feet again.

So Prescott, without in the least intending to let his prisoner get away, did not venture close enough to risk being pitched over on his back himself.

"Poor old skylarker, too! I'm sorry for him," muttered Dick, under his breath. "I'm afraid this spells trouble for some yearling."

"What can I do, though? I show my own unfitness if I let anyone run the guard past me."

"Call again, sentry on three!" directed the voice of Corporal Brodie.

"Here, sir," Dick answered.

Then to the spot ran the corporal, followed by two men of the guard.

"Two or more men attempted to cross this post, sir," Dick reported. "One tripped, and I'm holding him."

"Head him off, if he attempts to run ahead," directed Mr. Brodie, nodding to one of his men of the guard. "Now, then, get up, and let us see whether you're a cadet, or only a banker's son."

But the figure did not rise.

"Get up, sir, I tell you," ordered Corporal Brodie, slowly stepping past Prescott.

But the figure did not stir.

"Perhaps the man fell and stunned himself," muttered Brodie. Passing his rifle to his left hand the corporal parted the bushes, then bent over the prostrate one.

"Oh, hang you!" growled the cadet corporal. He seized the figure with his right hand, yanked it upward, then hurled it out, letting it fall again across the post.

"Is that the man you stopped, Mr. Prescott?" demanded Corporal Brodie in disgust.

But instead of answering, at that moment, Dick straightened up, brought his rifle to port, and hailed:

"Halt! Who's there?"

"The officer of the day," came out of the blackness.

"Advance, officer of the day, to be recognized," Dick replied.

Forward out of the deep shadow came Cadet Captain Reynolds.

"What's the trouble, Corporal?" inquired the latest arrival.

"Mr. Prescott reports that two or more persons attempted to run across his post, sir. He overtook one, who stumbled. Mr. Prescott was guarding his prisoner as I arrived, sir, and that was the prisoner!"

Corporal Hasbrouck pointed in disdain at the stuffed figure that he had hauled out from under the bushes and Dick's bayonet.

"A stuffed figure, in gray trousers and shirt, eh?" questioned Captain Reynolds. "Sentry, were the two or three men who got away from you of the same composition?"

"I don't know, sir," Dick answered, with mortification. "All I know, sir, is that those who got away ran pretty fast, and made so little noise that they doubtless wore rubber-soled shoes."

"You've been hoaxed, sentry," commented the officer of the day dryly. "Corporal, have your men of the guard bring the prisoner up to the guard tent. Sentry, if any more straw men attempt to cross your post, bring them down as well as you did this one. The straw men who got away from you made their way into camp, didn't they?"

"Whoever escaped, sir, got into camp all right."

As the guard-house party returned, Dick resumed the pacing of number three. He felt his face still blazing, from the quiet ridicule of the officer of the day.

"I'll catch it to-morrow from everyone who thinks me worth noticing," growled the plebe to himself. "However, though I tried to do my full duty, I'm glad that was what I caught. I wouldn't care to march a comrade in, a prisoner."

When the midnight relief came around, and Prescott's relief was posted in his place, the young plebe knew the ordeal ahead of him.

As soon as the relieved squad was halted at the guard tent, and Dick entered to get himself a cup of coffee and a sandwich or two, his glance fell upon the stuffed figure, which reposed on the floor at the back of the tent as though it had been a veritable prisoner.

"Did you shoot it, Prescott?" asked Derwent, the man who had just been relieved on number four.

"No; he lassoed it with his neck-tie," jeered another man of the guard.

"Wonder if the prisoner is hungry!" pursued Derwent. "Prescott, the prisoner is yours. Attend to his feeding. And the poor fellow should have some proper bedding, too, a chilly night like this."

"A merciful soldier wouldn't eat until he had seen his prisoner fed," tantalized another.

Dick had his cup of coffee at his mouth.

"Prescott, old man," commented fat Smith, "you'll be commended in general orders for distinguished bravery."

That was enough, in itself, to make Dick choke, but Smith emphasized his remark by slapping Dick on the back. An ounce of hot coffee, at least, "went down the wrong way." Choking and gasping for breath, trying to expel the coffee from his windpipe, and all the while obliged to lean well forward so as not to expel any of the coffee over the front of his blouse, Dick thought he never would get his breath again.

"Instead of feeding his prisoner, I believe Mr. Prescott has been eating some of his prisoner," observed Corporal Hasbrouck dryly. "Mr. Prescott, himself, appears to be full of straw at present."

The general laugh that followed didn't make it any easier for the victim of all this nonsense. In laughing again Dick choked so that he began to turn slightly black.

"Dry up, you hyenas!" ordered Cadet Captain Reynolds, as he rushed to Prescott's relief. In a few moments the late sentry on number three was breathing easily again. He threw himself down on a mattress, and was soon asleep.

But in the morning he had to go through the ordeal ten-fold. As Dick went to his tent to change some articles of clothing Bert Dodge appeared in the company street.

"Hey, mister," called yearling Davis, after Bert, "I hear good news. Last night the guard caught the chap who shanghaied you."

Even Greg and Anstey were prepared to quiz the "hero" of the comic episode of the night before.

"That was a fine comic opera performance, old chap," grinned Anstey.

"The next time you arrest a lay figure," suggested Greg, "at least be good enough to capture one that's stuffed with lemons."

"Oh, the straw figure was a lemon, of a kind," laughed the Virginian.

"Did the prisoner yell when you pricked point of your bayonet in its flesh of husks?" Greg wanted to know.

"Do you expect the K.C. to mention you in orders for distinguished gallantry?" demanded Anstey.

"Or to skin you on a suspicion of stealing straw from the artillery stables?" snickered Greg.

"I know one funny thing about straw, anyway," declared Anstey, turning around to Holmes.

"What?" asked Greg.

"It's bound to tickle you," declared the Virginian gravely.

Even at breakfast, in the cadet mess, Dick failed to get away from his tormentors. One of the yearlings, seated at a table not far from the one at which Prescott sat, called out to a classmate:

"Queer thing about that prisoner bagged on number three last night. Did you hear who the prisoner turned out to be?"

"No-o-o," drawled the other yearling, while a hundred pairs of eyes were turned on flame-faced Prescott.

"It was the class president of the beasts" (plebes).

"Kind of tough fate for the prisoner, though," railed another.

"What's that?"

"He's been sentenced to death. He is to be used as a target for the plebe squads in target practice."

"That isn't a sentence of death; it's a guarantee of safety."

This last sally turned the laugh on the entire plebe class. Dick flushed worse than ever when he saw many of his classmates begin to squirm.

"They might, at least, take it all out on me, and leave the class alone," muttered Dick to himself.

"Where are you going so fast, mister?" hailed a yearling, after the return to camp, as he beheld a plebe hurrying down a company street.

"I'm summoned as a witness before the general court-martial," called back Mr. Plebe, over his shoulder.

"Court-martial? I hadn't heard there was to be one."

"Yes, sir; they're going to try the prisoner caught on number three, sir."

The yearling turned away grinning, for once not deeming it necessary to rebuke a "beast" for attempting to make a smart answer.

Out on the range, at target practice, two mornings later, Dick did some especially bad shooting.

"Don't be afraid of hitting the target, Mr. Prescott," advised Lieutenant Gerould dryly. "It's made of something more substantial than straw."

A gleeful roar went up from some of the other "beasts." Lieutenant Gerould eyed them in surprise, for this Army officer was one of the few at West Point who had not already heard of number three sentry's capture.

It was a fortnight ere Cadet Prescott could feel really secure against more "joshing" over the incident.

"I'm better satisfied than if we had done what we set out to do to that plebe," remarked Yearling Davis to his tentmates.

"Mr. Prescott is a rather decent sort - for a mere plebe," replied Poultney. "Do you know, I think he's almost glad that he caught the dummy we rigged for him. I believe the little beast would have hated to catch a uniform stuffed with human flesh."

CHAPTER XIV

POOR GREG CAN'T EXPLAIN

The weeks slipped by, though not without the friction of sincerely hard work.

Dick, Greg and many of their classmates, toiling, marching, drilling under the hot sun that shone on the West Point plain and drill areas, acquired deep coats of manly tan on faces, necks and hands.

In many a story of West Point life the summer encampment is made to appear "the good old summer time" of an Army career. The West Point cadet knows better. It is a season of the hardest work.

At an hour when most city-dwelling boys are turning over in bed for another long and luxurious "snooze" the West Point cadet is up and doing in earnest.

There is much instruction that the young man has to absorb. Merely to take part is not enough. The young man must make himself proficient in such branches of the soldier's art as cavalry tactics, drill, horsemanship, scouting, artillery tactics and drill, with drill at the guns of different calibers, and target practice with field, siege, mountain, mortar, howitzer and seacoast guns, with a lot of work in the service of mines.

Infantry tactics, with unceasing drill and a lot of target

practice, provide a great amount of work.

Then there is a wide range of work to be mastered in practical military engineering, with the building of field fortifications, obstacles, spar and trestle bridges, pontoon bridges, military reconnoissance and sketching, map-making, surveying, military signaling and telegraphy, wireless and telephone service, the making of war material, the managing and handling of pack trains, field manoeuvres, and - well, it's not a season of ideal play!

It was toward the end of this busy season of outdoor life that Greg got into his most serious trouble up to that time, with an upper class man.

The day had been unusually hot, even for West Point. Those of the upper class men who felt the call to the evening's hop had dressed with utmost care and departed for the ballroom and the glances of soft eyes.

An unusually large number, however, were in camp this evening.

Tattoo sounds at 9.30. Men who wish are privileged to make up their beds and turn in at this hour. Greg was among the large number who went to sleep soon after tattoo this sultry night. For that matter, young Holmes was lonely, both Dick and Anstey having been drawn for guard duty.

Five minutes after tattoo Yearlings Davis and Poultney sauntered down the company street.

"Suzz-zz! suzz-zz! Horwack!" came sonorously from the tent solely occupied by Plebe Holmes.

"Great Washington!" muttered Poultney. "Who smuggled a sawmill into camp?"

"The disturbance of the peace comes from this abode of

beasts," declared Mr. Davis, halting and thrusting his head into the tent.

Greg did not awaken, but snored on with crescendo effects.

"We ought to teach a beast like that a lesson," whispered Poultney, as he, also, stared in at the unconscious but offending Greg.

"How?"

A hurried, whispered conference followed. Right after that Mr. Davis tied a stout cord to the tent-pole of the khaki house across the company street. Four feet of this cord were supported, in the crotches of two imbedded twigs, so that the cord lay about an inch and a half above the ground for a space of four feet close to the opposite tent. Then the balance of the cord was allowed to lie harmless across the company street. The end of the cord these two resourceful yearlings tied to a noose. Tiptoeing into Greg's tent they slipped the noose over one of Greg's forefingers.

If, within the next few minutes, any passersby used that company street, they plainly must have passed on Greg's side of the thoroughfare, and thus have avoided fouling with the cord.

Cadets who "drag femmes" to hop, and who have to escort their fair partners to hotel, or to some officer's house on the post, must go from Cullum Hall with their fair charges, leave them at the destined gate, and then return to camp, all within a stated, scheduled time.

The time it properly takes to walk from Cullum Hall to the hotel grounds, or to any officer's house, is all scheduled and kept track of at the guard tent. The young man thus returning to camp after taps reports to what building he escorted his "femme," and the time of his return is noted on the guard report. If the cadet has overstayed his time he is called to account for it the next day.

Yearling Butler had "dragged" this evening. He made guard tent on time, after a quick walk back to camp. Reporting, Mr. Butler saw the time noted by the amanuensis of the guard.

Then, feeling really sleepy, the yearling continued at a rather brisk walk to the head of his company street, and turned down.

Just as luck would have it Mr. Butler did not pass on Greg's side of the street, but passed rather close to the tent opposite.

Certainly the yearling's eyes were not on the ground. He saw not the cord on this side of the street.

There was a catch, a trip, and Mr. Butler went to the ground, mussing the knees of his spooniest pair of white ducks. Moreover, he cut the palm of his right hand, slightly, on a sharp pebble.

The pulling on the cord gave Greg's right hand a sharp yank, awakening the innocent plebe.

But Mr. Butler, having swiftly discovered the cord, and having ascertained in what direction it ran, made a dive into the tent just in time to see Greg sitting up on his mattress, holding the cord.

"So, mister," gruffed the yearling, "is this the way you amuse yourself late at night?"

"Why - what -" stammered Cadet Holmes.

"Now, don't try any of that on me," urged Mr. Butler angrily. "Mister, you're caught with the freight in your possession. What are you holding that cord for, sir?"

"I - I don't know, sir," quavered Greg, who was just beginning to feel awake after his rudely disturbed slumber.

"You - don't - know!" retorted Mr. Butler, in high dudgeon.

"What - what has happened, sir?" inquired Greg.

To Mr. Butler this seemed very much like adding insult to injury.

"You thought it was funny, did you, mister, to rig a cord across the company street?" raged the yearling, though he kept his voice down to a gentlemanly pitch. "You play tricks like that on upper class men. Of all the b.j. imps that ever put on gray! Mister, all I'm sorry for is that the officer of the day, or the O.C. didn't trip over your cord! Or the K.C. himself!"

"Now, I want to understand this, sir," contended Cadet Holmes, rising from his mattress and stepping forward. "I've just been aroused out of a sound sleep, and I find myself with a cord tied to one of my fingers."

"Oh, you do, mister?" jeered Mr. Butler harshly.

"And you, sir, come into this tent and accuse me of something. What I am anxious to know, sir, is what it is that I am accused of."

"See here, mister, I've no more time to waste on a b.j. beast. You've spoiled my best white ducks, and, incidentally, my temper. You compound this by adding more b.j.-ety. If you don't know what I'm going to do about it, wait until you hear from me, mister!"

Turning, very erect and stiff, in his outraged dignity, Mr. Butler left the tent.

"Now, what on earth have I done, anyway?" wondered Greg.

In his perplexity he stepped to the doorway of his tent. He saw the business-like arrangement of the cord, and all was clear to him, now.

"Some hazer has rigged that cord and tied one end to my finger," gasped Plebe Holmes.

Then a grin overspread his face.

"Well, it was mighty clever, anyway."

An instant more, and the grin gave place to a serious look.

"Clever or not, it certainly spells trouble for me."

When the cadets returned from breakfast in the morning, and while Greg was finishing the donning of field uniform for a forenoon of drill, a shadow fell across the doorway of the tent.

Prescott and Anstey were still members of the guard, and therefore absent.

"Mr. Holmes, I wish to speak with you," announced Mr. Haldane, of the yearling class.

"Will you come in, sir?"

Haldane stepped just inside the tent, standing severely erect and gazing coldly at the plebe.

"Mr. Butler demands a fight with you, mister, and as early as possible."

There was no mention of possible apology. Evidently Mr. Butler considered the affair one that could be remedied only by blows.

"Mr. Haldane, I don't wish to ask much delay. But the two friends whom I shall want to represent me are on guard duty at present. May I ask that you see Mr. Prescott?"

"Very good," acknowledged Mr. Haldane, and left the tent.

"Now, I'm in for it," muttered Greg ruefully. "And the queer part of it is that I have to fight for a thing that I never did. But I'm not going to make any denials now, unless Dick advises it."

It was evening, after the cadets had returned from supper, when Mr. Haldane appeared and asked for Prescott. The two stepped outside together, walking a little distance away to make the necessary arrangements.

Dick was already in possession of the few facts that Greg had to tell him. Dick had advised against denying the prank, for the present, anyway.

"It would look like playing the baby act," Prescott had explained to his chum, and in this view Anstey agreed.

Mr. Haldane and Dick came to a speedy understanding. The fight was to take place the next morning, at the first peep of daylight.

Promptly, however, the affair became noised about through camp.

Butler was a considerably larger man than Greg, and looked in every way more powerful. Cadet Corporal Atwater, who was president of the yearling class, went to see Mr. Butler promptly.

"At least, Butler, if you insist that the fight must be fought, let the scrap committee choose one of our class who is down nearer to the plebe's size," urged Mr. Atwater.

"Under ordinary conditions, old fellow, I'd be tickled to do it," replied Mr. Butler. "But, in a trick of this kind, I couldn't get any satisfaction out of anyone else hammering the b.j. beast who put up such a tumble for me."

"I'm thinking the scrap committee may interfere with your plans," rejoined Atwater, shaking his head. "We don't want fighting to degenerate into the appearance of bullying oppression of beasts."

"I'll have to abide by the decision of the scrap committee, of course," admitted Butler. "But I hope the fellows won't interfere."

Cadet Corporal Atwater promptly called the scrap committee together. Many newspaper writers, through ignorance, have condemned the existence of a scrap committee at West Point, claiming that it foments fights. The truth is that the scrap committee is a court of honor, formed for adjusting nice questions, and for preventing unfair fighting.

Cadet Butler was summoned before the scrap committee, and stated his case. The decision of the scrap committee was that a fight would have to take place, but that Mr. Holmes was privileged to request the scrap committee to name a yearling who was Holmes's own size and weight, this substitute to fight in Mr. Butler's place at once.

Cadet Corporal Atwater thereupon promptly called at Greg's tent, and stated the decision to the three tentmates.

"Mr. Prescott will answer for me, sir," Greg replied respectfully.

"Sir," Dick answered, "we appreciate the decision of the scrap committee. We recognize that we are being used with the utmost fairness, and that all Mr. Holmes's rights are being safeguarded in the most honorable manner. Yet, sir, this fight has a peculiar basis. More so than with most fights, I believe, sir, this is a purely personal one. Mr. Holmes, therefore, is prepared, sir, to give personal satisfaction. While the odds are very distinctly against him, he wishes to show that he can take his trouncing like a cadet and a gentleman. So, sir, with renewed assurances of our thanks and appreciation, Mr.

Holmes is ready to meet Mr. Butler at daylight."

"That is well spoken, sir," replied Mr. Atwater. "I appreciate the grit of Mr. Holmes's decision."

The president of the yearling class went back to acquaint Mr. Butler with the outcome.

Until close of taps Greg practiced various blows, feints and dodges in foot work.

"You can't win, Greg," advised Anstey. "Of course that's out of the question. But, before you have to lose the count you want to make sure of giving Mr. Butler enough facial decorations to keep him satisfied for some time to come."

At taps the three tentmates lay down on their mattresses, Dick with an alarm clock close to his hand.

Cadets Prescott and Anstey were soon sound asleep. Greg, however, lay awake for a long time, thinking - thinking.

"If I had some of Dick's lightning speed, and his capacity for sailing in like a cyclonic fury," thought Greg. "Whew, but I wish I had always given more attention to boxing than I have done. I will after this."

Finally, Greg dozed off. The next he knew was when a brief, metallic "br-r-r-r?" sounded in the tent. In another instant Dick had the clock and was smothering the noise. Greg Holmes leaped up. It was the morning of his fight!

CHAPTER XV

GREG OVERHEARS A PRETTY GIRL'S TRIBUTE

In the tent it was still dark. It was at the fag-end of the night; the time which, as military commanders know, most tries men's bravery.

The latter part of the night had been cool. Now, in the brief space before dawn the air was positively chilly.

Greg shivered.

Perhaps it was the chill of the air. It is also extremely likely that Greg Holmes dreaded the conflict that was about to come off with big Butler.

Be that as it may, Cadet Holmes went on briskly with his dressing. The bravest man is he who, though afraid, goes straight ahead to the goal of battle despite his fears.

Greg was more sensitive about blows than was his chum. Until he got into the heat of action Cadet Holmes dreaded the very idea of giving or taking a blow. There are many soldiers like this; but when they get into action they are the bravest of the brave.

Dick and Anstey were also getting themselves swiftly in readiness. To Dick, veteran of three West Point fights, the greatest cause for regret seemed to lie in being robbed of some of their much-needed sleep.

In almost no time, so it seemed, three cadets fully attired in uniform, stole cautiously from the tent, slipping down the company street.

Dick carried Greg's fighting clothes. Cadet Anstey carried a bucket in which lay a sponge.

Whether cadet sentries on guard deliberately aid in letting fight parties slip across a post it would be impossible to say. Certain it is that Mr. Prescott, in the lead, reconnoitred carefully, then crossed the post at the point furthest from the sentry's half-audible footsteps. His two friends slipped over with him.

The faint gray of earliest dawn was just showing through the trees when the plebe trio came in sight of the famous hollow below old Fort Clinton.

Here already paced Mr. Plympton and Mr. Connors of the first class. They were to take charge of the affair.

"Good morning, mister," nodded Mr. Plympton to Dick, as Prescott came in sight at the head of his party. Greg and Anstey came in for no particular notice from the first class men.

"Hullo, But!"

"Hullo, old Conjunction!"

These were the greetings that Butler received when he appeared, followed by Haldane and Post. These young men, being yearlings, were actually human beings. At least, that was the way the plebes felt.

Now the stripping began rapidly. Each principal drew on a sleeveless jersey and gymnasium trousers, the latter secured by a belt. On the feet were rubber-soled shoes, as giving the best chance for foothold on the damp ground.

The seconds began kneading the muscles of their principals, and otherwise putting them in shape.

Mr. Butler yawned two or three times, appearing slightly bored. Greg did not glance in the direction of his coming antagonist, but Holmes's face was impassive, inscrutable. He did not appear nervous. The moment had come, and Greg faced the situation dumbly but absolutely without fear.

Then the principals were placed in their corners. Referee Plympton stated the terms under which the meeting was to be held. Then at the call, the two cadets leaped forward.

"Remember the moves we planned last night," had been Dick's last whispered words.

On Butler's face rested a broad grin. He pranced about lightly, swinging his hardmuscled arms. He intended to start with a bit of easy nonsense, putting Holmes off his guard. Then the yearling's plan was to make the affair a lesson in scientific mauling.

While Butler was dancing about, grinning, Greg, vastly more watchful than he appeared to be, suddenly let his right out in a feint, then followed with a left drive.

Butler all but struck this blow up, yet, as he darted back from the parry, the yearling tasted blood from his own lower lip. That taught him that even a despised little plebe like Mr. Holmes might have his points of danger.

"Now, stand up and let us see how good your quick counter is," laughed the yearling, dancing about.

Butler's footwork was fine and fast, but Greg, watching him, only pivoted about, putting up his hands with great speed.

Thus Greg blocked all but three or four lighter blows up to the time when the time-keeper's interruption came.

"You won't need to do much in the rubbing line," whispered Greg, as his seconds started in on him in his "corner." "My man, as yet, hasn't any more than warmed me up."

"Look out for a smash on the nose, old fellow," warned Dick. "You got first blood in a half-sort of way, by that cut on the other man's lip. In this next round Mr. Butler will try to get the real first blood."

"I hope so," muttered Greg dreamily. "For that one I believe I have one of the best counters known."

Surely enough, in the beginning of the second round, Butler feinted, then led off for a hard one on the plebe's nose. But the delivery was the very one that Cadet Holmes wanted. He ducked, feinted, and slammed in just above Mr. Butler's belt with such force that the big yearling staggered. Yet Butler was a wary fighter; he blocked Greg's follow-up scheme, then fought for time. Towards the end of the round, however, Butler again tried for the plebe's nose. This time he failed again, but Greg's counter-blow landed on the point of a shoulder. Butler would have been away in another instant, but Greg's right came out of a hook and tapped the yearling emphatically on the end of his nose. As the yearling fought back furiously the blood spurted from his nose.

Then, just before time was called, Greg got his left eye too much in line with the yearling's right fist.

Dazed, Cadet Holmes was saved only by the word from the time-keeper. Had the round lasted fifteen seconds more Mr. Butler would have had the plebe out.

Erect, and as jauntily went back to his corner. [Transcriber's note: missing text?]

"I reckon you've got as a bad looking window here," murmured Anstey sympathetically, as he swabbed at the damaged surface around the eye. "Make it short, Holmesy, or you're going to meet with more damage, I reckon."

"This is the last serious smash that Greg is going to take," put in Dick coolly. "In the third he's going to remember the old Gridley fighting principle: Greg, you simply can't be whipped. Now, wade in and seize hold of Mr. Butler's scalp-lock."

Soon the fighters were at it again. Two or three body blows Greg took, and they stung, coming from such steam-driven fists as the yearling's. But Mr. Holmes's damaged left eye was closing rapidly. He was forced to squint through that eye, getting most of his sight through the right. Of course, the yearling, who now realized he had something more than a dummy to fight, manoeuvred at Greg's left side after that.

The third round was drawing to a close. Butler landed one on the side of young Holmes's head that sent the plebe spinning. Yet, as he swung, Greg dropped a hard blow on Mr. Butler's already damaged nose. There was a gasp of pain from the yearling.

"Time!" called Mr. Connors.

Greg went back to his seconds, a good deal jarred, his wind troubled, and his left eye rapidly assuming a most ugly look. One more really good one from the larger fighter would put the plebe out of the affair.

"Be cool, now, old chap," admonished Dick in an undertone, as he and Anstey worked over their comrade. "The next round probably decides it."

"Cool!" grimaced Cadet Holmes. "Why, I guess I am every-where except in my punished eye. That feels like a red-hot furnace!"

As the men faced each other for the fourth round Greg, through his right eye, saw a look of intent in Butler's eye that meant business. The yearling was now going in, in earnest, to wind up this affair.

"I'm going to get something out of this!" grumbled Cadet Holmes inwardly.

As Butler came at him, swift and terrible, Cadet Holmes formed the purpose of playing off a block to be followed by a direct and sure assault on one of his man's eyes. And presently the chance came. Greg bounced in so resolutely over Butler's right eye that the yearling staggered back, fighting for sight and wind. But Greg, who knew it was thrash-or-be-thrashed, was merciless. He leaped about, harassing his opponent, then sent in a well-calculated blow that closed the yearling's other eye.

Butler reeled. It looked as though he must go down. Greg, unwilling to take any unfair advantage, paused a second. Then, realizing that Mr. Butler was keeping his feet, Cadet Holmes leaped in, feinting blow after blow with such speed that the yearling was dazed. Suddenly, with a new feint for the yearling's solar plexus, Holmes suddenly raised, driving in hard on the left side of Mr. Butler's jaw. That sent the dazed man down. He went in a heap, then unfolded and lay limp.

Time-keeper Connors began to count, though perfunctorily. There was no reason to believe that Mr. Butler could wake up in time, and he didn't. Mr. Plympton, in a cold tone, awarded the fight to the plebe. Butler's seconds went to work over him, but it was some minutes before they brought him back to consciousness. By this time Greg was dressed.

"Mr. Butler," murmured Greg, bending over his at last conscious opponent, "I would like to say a word - now. That business with the cord was a trick put up on me, not on you. You were only the incidental victim. I had no willing or knowing part in your discomfiture. I tell you this now, sir, after having proved that I wasn't afraid merely of being called out. I am tremendously sorry that this fight had to be."

"You held up your end all right, mister," was the yearling's concise tribute.

Then, after sending Anstey back to camp with the officials, Dick accompanied Greg to cadet hospital, where the latter's eye was dressed and "painted out" as much as could be.

Both of Mr. Butler's seconds were required to help him to hospital. Nor did the yearling get out very soon. His jaw had not been fractured, but for some days the medical officers feared "green-stick" fracture, with a consequent danger of suppuration. It was not until after the end of the encampment that the yearling was discharged from hospital.

"Where's Mr. Butler to-night?" inquired a very pretty girl, as she strolled through camp in the evening, between two attentive yearlings. She was the same whom Butler had last accompanied to a hop.

"Mr. Butler is in hospital," replied Mr. McGraw.

"Yes, and pounded to such a pulp that his mother wouldn't know him," laughed a young "cit.," the girl's cousin. "Over there is Holmes, the plebe who did it."

"What a disgusting brute Mr. Holmes must be!" muttered the girl indignantly, and Greg, hearing her, colored violently, but could not reply. Plebes are not allowed the acquaintance of the young ladies.

CHAPTER XVI

TAPS SOUNDS ON SUMMER

Cadet Dodge spent the last days of the encampment on sick report.

He got word that Mr. Poultney was one of the yearlings concerned in his discomfiture on post number three, and boldly confronted the yearling with the charge.

In the fight that followed Dodge received a fearful walloping from Mr. Poultney.

The laws of courtesy are enforced by these fights. A new man, entering the United States Military Academy, often has a most exaggerated idea of his own importance and merits. In some instances the new cadet is likely to disregard the rights of upper class men. A fight puts the offending plebe where he belongs. Further, the knowledge that he will have to fight for every serious infraction of the rules of courtesy results in quickly making a disciplined soldier and considerate gentleman out of the cadet who is inclined to be bumptious.

In the training of personal character it may readily be believed that the cadet's plebe year, with its "chalk-line" and repression, is worth all the rest of the time spent at West Point.

Milk-sops and peace-at-any-price advocates may as well turn their attention away from West Point. These ultra-peaceable ones, who long for the promotion of peace through the abolition of all armies, have at hand an experiment that can be carried out only on a smaller scale.

Let these peace-at-any-price agitators, in a given community, set about to stamp out crime by abolishing the police force! An army is merely a force of international policemen.

*   *   *   *   *   *

In the last days of August the furloughed new second class returned. The young men, after reporting at the adjutant's office at the required hour, formed and marched to camp, still in "cit." clothes.

First and third class men rushed out to receive and congratulate the returned travelers, while the plebes stood shyly by. Their welcome was not wanted. Then the second class men disappeared into their tents. They were out again, quickly enough, in white ducks and the cadet gray blouses. They had taken up the cadet life for two years more. In the afternoon these second class men swelled the ranks of the battalion and went through, with all the old-time fervor, the grand old ceremony of dress parade.

That night came the "Show." This annual show at the end of August may be either the Camp Illumination or the Color Line Entertainment. This year the class presidents had asked for the latter.

As soon as dark came on, the Color Line - the central line through cadet camp - blazed out with lights. Soon after the band began to play gayly. Hundreds of visitors, most of them women, and the majority quite young women, flocked to camp. Along the color line the guns of the battalion were stacked. Over the center of the line the colors of the country and the cadet colors were draped with beautiful effect. Cadets of the three upper classes escorted the visitors through. The plebes stood by their own tents, answering when spoken to, which was not often.

After the band had played several selections the musicians moved up before a hastily constructed stage. Plays or musical farces, written and acted by cadets, are often presented. In Dick's plebe summer, however, the choice had been for a minstrel show.

Half an hour before the opening of the performance thirty of the cadets vanished to a big dressing tent behind the stage.

Before the stage hundreds of seats had been arranged. Every cadet who escorted ladies was privileged to sit with them. Cadets who "stagged" it were expected to stand. All of the plebes were in this number.

Presently the cadets, their faces blacked, came out of the dressing tent, taking their places off the stage. A regulation first part was now provided, with the aid of the band playing as an orchestra. In style it was the minstrel first part with which we are all familiar. There was this difference: The jokes hit off exclusively local affairs and conditions. The officers who served as instructors at West Point did not by any means escape in the running fire of minstrelsy nonsense.

Then came forth a woeful figure, blackfaced and attired in a dilapidated uniform. As he turned sideways it was noted that this cadet, who was really a rollicking second class man, wore on his back a card labeled in large letters:

"Plebe. Please don't mistreat."

At first sight of the pitiable object a roar of laughter went up from the spectators. Nowhere was the laughter louder than in the ranks of the standing plebes themselves, at the rear of the audience. This woeful-looking performer, after the orchestra had played a few preliminary strains, launched into a parody of "Nobody Loves Me." The song was full of hits on the b.j. "beast." The real plebes [Transcriber's note: missing text] with keen enjoyment.

"Mr. Plescott!" called the interlocutor, after the song and two encore verses had been sung.

"Yes, sah," falteringly replied the minstrel plebe, turning awkwardly and saluting with the wrong hand.

Though the name called was "Plescott," half of the plebe class turned to grin at Cadet Richard Prescott.

Dick stood it well, waiting to see what the performer would next say.

"Mr. Plescott," continued the interlocutor, "I heard something said about you this morning that I didn't in the least like."

"Ye-e-es, sah?" inquired the minstrel plebe falteringly.

"I consider it, Mr. Plescott, a most insulting thing that I heard said about you."

"Ye-e-es, sah?" faltered the performer, his knees shaking and his eyes rolling in apprehension.

"Mr. Plescott, your defamer said you were not fit to eat with Hottentot savages! I had to call the fellow down severely. Think of it, Mr. Plescott - you not fit to eat with Hottentot savages."

"Dat was a mighty mean thing to say, sah. Mought ah ask what yo' said to de gemmun?"

"I told your defamer, Mr. Plescott, that he was entirely in error in asserting that you are not fit to eat with Hottentot savages. I assured him that you were!"

There was a wild whoop of glee from the spectators, especially from the other plebes, and Dick, though he laughed heartily, reddened when he found himself focused by so many scores of eyes.

Then the singer dropped off into another song, and the nonsense went on. After the first part came an olio in which were some fine singing, dancing, juggling and other work.

The performance came to an end in time for the cadets and their visitors to take another stroll through camp.

Bang! Bang! Bang! A glow and a burst of red fire! There was a bewildering maze of pyrotechnics. After five minutes of this the fireworks ceased, and, though the camp lights still burned the contrast seemed almost like darkness.

The members of the band rose. As the leader's baton fell the notes of "The Star Spangled Banner" rose triumphant on the night air. It was a glorious sight as a hundred Army officers and five hundred United States cadets clicked their heels, stood instantly at attention, uncovered their heads and stood with caps held over their hearts.

As the strains died out there was an impressive pause. Then, in lighter vein, the band rollicked out with the old, familiar, "Good Night Ladies," and, laughing merrily, the visitors departed, their cadet friends going with them only as far as camp limits.

Out on the plains beyond the visitors again halted for a brief instant.

In front of the guard tent a drummer sounded "taps" - three strokes on the drum. All but the authorized lights in guard tent and O.C.'s tent were extinguished.

The summer encampment was over.

"Oh, dear!" sighed many a fair visitor as she returned to a sheltering roof. "The summer's fun is over. To-morrow these splendid young men will be back in barracks, grilling and boning for their very lives!"

H. Irving Hancock

CHAPTER XVII

MR. DODGE GOES CANVASSING

Yes, the good old summer time was over. Bending over study tables in cadet barracks the young men pored over books and papers of their own making.

The first few days seemed fearfully hard. To the young men who had been for weeks away from their books it seemed for a while all but impossible to pick up the threads of study in a way that would anything like satisfy the Army officers who acted as their relentless instructors.

"Relentless?" To the average boy in grammar or high school it does not seem like a hardship to be required to make a percentage of at least sixty-six and two-thirds per cent. in all studies. In the public schools it seems rather easy to reach that kind of an average.

At West Point the markings are on a scale of three, with decimal shadings. A man who secures in any study a marking of two is deemed proficient. If his average marking in a term is 2.6, he is rather highly proficient in that study. A marking of two on a scale of three is equivalent to sixty-six and two-thirds per cent., and this does not seem, to the outsider, a difficult attainment. But the West Point speed of study! In a high school the young man is given the whole of the first year in which to qualify in simple algebra; in the second year he takes up plane geometry; in the third he comes upon solid geometry;

in the fourth year of high school work the young man masters plane trigonometry and solves allied problems.

At West Point, in the plebe year, the young man, in the first half of the year, goes through simple algebra and plane and solid geometry. In the second half of the year he must force his way understandingly through advanced algebra and plane and spherical trigonometry! This is his mathematics work merely for the first year, yet it is more and more thoroughly covered than the high school boy's entire course.

During their first three months of plebedom, and with their course behind them in the really fine high school at Gridley, Dick and Greg had not found their math. much of a torment. But now, after coming back from encampment, these young men began to wake up to the fact that West Point mathematics is a giant contrasted with the pigmy of public school mathematics. The two chums began to put in every minute they could spare over the long, bewildering array of problems assigned for each recitation.

"What a curious delusion we had, back at Gridley!" laughed Greg, in their room, one night.

"Which particular delusion was that!" Dick demanded, without looking up from his geometry.

"Why, we thought our easy old Gridley work in math. was going to fit us to race easily through the first two years here!"

"That isn't the only pipe that has burned out in our pockets since we became plebes!" grunted Dick.

"Are you going to max it (get a high marking) in math, to-morrow, old fellow?"

"I'm going to 'fess out (fail) more likely," sighed Dick. "How are you coming on, general?"

H. Irving Hancock

"I'd give a good deal to be able to ask a first class man how to solve the fourth problem on to-morrow's list," groaned Greg.

"I'd show you," sighed Dick, "only I'm afraid I might lead you into an ambush where you'd get scalped by the instructor."

In each class, and in every subject of study, the young men are divided, for recitation purposes, into sections of eight or ten men. In each study the section to which the young man belongs is determined by his relative standing in that study. The "banner" section is made up of the cadets who stand highest in the class in that particular study. At the end of every week the markings of each cadet in every one of his studies is posted, and the sections are rearranged, if need be. The men in the lowest section of all in a given study are styled the "goats." The members of the "goat" section, in math. for instance, are men who feel rather certain that they will presently be "found" and dropped from the cadet corps. However, at the beginning of a year a man may fall into the "goats," and then later, may pull up so that he reaches a higher section and goes on with better standing. But in general the "goats" are looked upon as men who are going to be dropped, and this usually applies, also, to a majority of the men in the two or three sections just above the "goats."

About forty per cent. of the young men who enter West Point as cadets are dropped before their course is over. Most of these losses occur in the plebe and yearling classes. When a man has completed two years at West Point he has a very good chance to get through and win his commission as an officer in the Army.

In geometry Greg was in the third section above the "goats," Dick in the sixth.

"I wish I had your head, old ramrod!" groaned Greg, half an hour later.

"If I should lose even a hair's weight from my head I'd be in the 'goats' next week," replied Prescott grimly. "If I ever get to be an officer in the Army, I wonder what earthly good all these math. headaches will do me in handling a bunch of raw rookies?"

"If we have to go back to Gridley, 'skinned,'" grimaced Greg, "we'll at least have company. Dodge is only a tenth above 'goat' grade in geom., and next week will probably see him there."

"And he was considered a good student in Gridley!" quoth Dick sadly.

That Dodge, however, still had hopes of being able to hold on was proved by the fact that he was now conducting a vigorous campaign for election to the class presidency.

"I think I am as good as elected class president," he wrote home to the elder Dodge. And, the next time Theodore Dodge went over to his bank in Gridley, Theodore Dodge circulated the news among his intimates. The evening "Mail," in Gridley, came out with the statement that Dodge was sure to become class president.

"And thus Gridley will have cause to feel that it occupies no small place of honor, after all, in national affairs," penned the editor of the "Mail."

Dodge had a rather fair following of friends in the class, since he had become modest enough to drop his pretensions to caste and extra social position and they were working hard for him.

That young man came early to Dick and Greg, asking them to work for him.

"I don't quite care to pledge myself," Dick replied kindly. "When the class meeting is called I'd rather go in with a free mind on the subject. Then, Dodge, if I consider you the best man put in nomination, I'll vote for you."

Though this was not a positive assurance Dodge and his campaign managers made use of it to put Dick's name in the list of supporters.

One evening, at dress parade, when the cadet adjutant read the day's orders, he came to this announcement:

"Members of the fourth class are requested to meet, under permission of the Superintendent, at the Y.M.C.A. at eight o'clock to-night, for the election of a class president, and for transaction of such other business as may properly come before the meeting. Members of the upper classes will accordingly remain away from the Y.M.C.A. to-night."

"Remember, you fellows," called Bert Dodge, thrusting his head into Dick and Greg's room after return to barracks, "I count upon your strong support to-night."

CHAPTER XVIII

THE PLEBE CLASS CHOOSES ITS PRESIDENT

Not a man save two on sick report at cadet hospital was absent when Cadet Hopper, acting as temporary chairman, the plebe class called to order.

"Gentlemen," he announced, "you all know the principal reason for our being here. We are, in especial, to elect a class president. Therefore I will take time only to urge upon you the great importance of to-night's planned action.

"The class president is to be, in a word, the class leader. The president of this class is to stand before the entire cadet body, and before the authorities of the United States Military Academy, as the representative of this class.

"It goes without saying, I think, that our president should be, in every respect, the best possible representative of the class as a whole. He should be as nearly as possible the ideal man of the class - the man who stands for the best, the manliest and the most loyal thoughts and aspirations of this class.

"As brevity is always highly to be prized, I will say no more at this moment. If any gentleman present desires to address the class, I will recognize him for that purpose. If, after a pause, we ascertain that no member desires to make a general address, I will then rule that the election is next in order."

"Mr. Chairman!"

"Mr. Lawrence."

"I believe, Mr. Chairman," cried Mr. Lawrence, "that I have never heard the objects or the duty of a meeting better expressed, or in fewer words. I am certain that I voice the sense of this class meeting when I say that the thanks of the plebe class are due to the chairman. I have only to add my own personal, urgent appeal that the man chosen for the greatest honor we can bestow be truly a man who represents the best that there is in this class. And now, Mr. Chairman, I move that we proceed at once to nominations."

"Nominations with speeches?" asked the chairman.

"Yes, Mr. Chairman."

"I second the motion, as amended," declared Cadet Thompson.

The motion was put and carried.

Cadets Hopper and Lawrence were both nominated, and the nominations seconded.

"Mr. Chairman!"

"Mr. Delavan."

Cadet Delavan was upon his feet, the recognized and avowed arch-supporter of Mr. Dodge. Delavan made an introductory appeal in which he brought forth and endorsed the remarks of the chair. He then brought forth, as leading characteristics in a wise and capable class president a high sense of honor, wide judgment, intimacy with the world and its social usages, and unswerving loyalty to country, the Military Academy and the class.

"In these and in all other essential and even ideal respects, Mr. Chairman, we have everything that can be asked for in Mr. Dodge. Mr. Chairman, I most earnestly and urgently place Mr. Dodge in nomination for the office of president of this class."

Then Hadley was on his feet at once. In a longer and more eloquent speech he seconded the nomination. Hadley possessed the gift of eloquence. As he proceeded in his remarks he convinced many, until now wavering, that Bert Dodge was the most available man for the great office. When Hadley sat down it was the general opinion that Dodge was about as good as elected.

There was a long pause. Then:

"Mr. Chairman!"

"Mr. Anstey."

The Virginian nodded to the chair, then looked slowly around at all the faces. It was some moments ere his voice was again heard. When he did speak it was in a low, clear voice that gradually increased in volume.

"Mr. Chairman, and fellow members of the fourth class," Anstey continued in soft accents, "it may, at first thought, seem almost treacherous that I should favor any comrade over my own roommate."

Bert Dodge flushed angrily, then paled.

"Believe me, sir and gentlemen, only a burning desire to see the best interests of the class served could nerve me to such a seeming lack of grace."

In the intense stillness that followed the noise that Bert Dodge made in shifting his feet on the floor sounded loud, indeed. Anstey was a trifle paler than usual, but he was working under an intense conviction, and the grit and dash of his Revolutionary forbears was quite sufficient to carry him on unswervingly to his goal of duty to the class.

"Against Mr. Dodge, sir and classmates, I have no word to offer. I will admit that he would make a good president of the class. In one study Mr. Dodge for a while stood so persistently among the goats as to hint at the possibility that he might not be with us long."

Bert flushed angrily.

"But, most fortunately," pursued Anstey, in the same soft, Southern voice, "Mr. Dodge has lately pulled himself up from among the goats, and is most likely to remain here at the Academy for the allotted period of four years.

"Yet, sir and classmates, the words of our temporary presiding officer have sunk deeply into my brain. We must choose the man who is most truly representative of the whole spirit, purpose and daring of the class. With all due and high respect, gentlemen, for my own roommate, I desire to bring forward for your consideration the one who, I feel certain, stands more closely than any of us to all the grand old traditions of intelligence, daring, loyalty, leadership, good fellowship and unfailing good judgment. The man I would nominate, sir, will, to my mind, lead this class as no class has been led at the Military Academy within the last generation or two."

Mr. Anstey paused, glancing at the faces in front.

"Name him!"

"Yes! Name him!"

"Mr. Chairman, and classmates," continued the Virginian, "I have the honor - and I assure you I feel it an honor to have made the discovery - I have the honor to place in nomination for the class presidency the name of that splendid fellow and soldier-at-heart - Mr. Prescott!"

Greg it was gave a whoop that started the cheering.

"You sneak!" muttered Dodge under his breath, trying to hide the fire that burned in his eyes as he looked again at Cadet Anstey. But five men caught the low-uttered word and it cost Dodge five votes.

"Further nominations are in order," suggested Chairman Hopper.

There was a long pause, after which it was moved, seconded and carried that the nominations be closed.

"The chair then directs," continued Mr. Hooper, "that Messrs. Gentry, Hawkes, Fletcher and Simmons serve as tellers. Voting will be by written ballot, on slips that will be supplied by the tellers."

Soon the tellers circulated again through the meeting, receiving the written ballots in their caps. These were brought forward to the table behind the platform desk and counted. Then, after securing the floor, teller Hawkes announced the result as follows:

"Whole number of votes cast, 122; necessary to choice, 61. Of these Mr. Dodge has received 48; Mr. Prescott, 39; Mr. Hopper, 19, and Mr. Lawrence, 16."

"No choice having been made by the majority voting," decided the chair, "the tellers will again distribute blank slips and another ballot will be cast."

The second balloting resulted in this layout:

Dodge, 52; Prescott, 40; Hopper, 16; Lawrence, 14.

"No choice having yet been made, a third balloting will be

H. Irving Hancock

necessary," ruled the chair.

"Mr. Chairman - one moment, please!"

"Mr. Lawrence."

"Mr. Chairman and classmates," went on Lawrence hastily, "I regret that I have not the silver tongue possessed by some who have spoken to-night. Did I possess such a precious thing I would know how to thank appropriately, perhaps, those who have favored me enough to vote for me. I do thank these friends, though not as I would wish I might. But I now respectfully ask all of my friends who have voted for me to vote with me, and cast their votes for Mr. Prescott."

"The chair wishes to withdraw its name from this contest, with a similar tribute of thanks," declared Mr. Hopper. "Yet, perhaps as temporary presiding officer, it will not be wholly proper for me to declare in favor of either of the remaining candidates."

Then the tellers distributed ballots again. There was a great deal of excitement in the air. Bert Dodge and Dick Prescott were the observed of many eyes. Again the ballots were taken up and counted.

"Gentlemen," announced Chairman Hopper, as one of the tellers handed him a slip, "Mr. Dodge has fifty votes and Mr. Prescott has seventy-two. Mr. Prescott is, therefore, elected president of this class."

"Mr. Chairman," cried Greg, leaping to his feet, "I move to make the election unanimous."

"Second the motion!" called half a dozen at once.

It was put to an aye-and-no vote and carried rousingly.

"The chair gladly relinquishes its temporary post to the one elected to fill it," announced Mr. Hopper.

Anstey, Greg and a dozen others gleefully escorted the class president to the platform.

Dick addressed the meeting in a quiet, low voice, but he heartily thanked the class for the honor it had accorded him.

"I'm not going to make a speech, gentlemen," he continued. "Perhaps a speech from me will be worth more when I am through with the office. But I have listened attentively to what has been outlined to-night by other speakers as constituting a worthy president, and I can only add that I shall do all that may possibly be in my power to live up to such ideals. The chair now stands ready to be advised of any further business that may properly come before the meeting."

There being no "business," the time was taken up with speeches from several plebes who wanted to be heard. The subject of their treatment by the yearlings came in for much attention. Many of the speakers expressed burning indignation at the "small show" accorded to the plebe class.

"Hasn't our president something to say on this subject?" called some one.

"I shall be glad to speak on this very matter," smiled Cadet Prescott, rising. "Gentlemen of the class, I know that we are traveling over a road that, even under the most genial conditions, would be a rough one. Many of us feel that the yearling class is devoting all its energies to making that road a still rougher one."

"Hear! Hear!" cried a dozen at once.

"But, gentlemen," continued the new class president, "next June we shall be yearlings. There will be a new lot of plebes here, and I feel rather certain that we shall treat them just about as we are now being treated."

There were murmurs of dissent at this.

"For generations," continued Cadet Prescott, "the plebe at West Point has had to rough it. You are all familiar with the truism that a soldier must learn to obey before he is fit for command. In much the same way, I fancy, the plebe must travel a rough road before he is thoroughly broken in and fitted to enjoy the delights of full equality and recognition with upper class men.

"We are no more put upon than was every present upper class man during his first year here. When we reach the sublime heights on which the yearlings dwell I believe that we shall look back and appreciate the fact that we truly needed some round thrashing into shape. We shall feel grateful to our present enemies, the yearlings - and we will turn around and help the new lot of plebes through the same kind of first-year life. In the meantime, classmates, I earnestly advise that we establish at least one record here. Let us, from now on, prove ourselves to be the gamest of plebes who have suffered here in many a year. The more patiently we bear it now, in all patience, the better yearlings, the better second class men and first class men we shall be when our time comes. The motto of a famous sovereign is, 'I serve.' Let our plebe class motto be, 'I grin and bear.'"

This wasn't exactly what the plebes had been expecting from their new leader. For a few moments after Dick sat down there was silence. Then a half dozen began to applaud. The noise grew, until half the plebes were cheering.

"Thank you, gentlemen," smiled the class president. "I think we are now well started on the way to becoming useful members of the Army."

"What do you think of our new leader?" one of Bert Dodge's late supporters asked that young man after the meeting had broken up.

"We're going to have a boot-lick president," growled Bert.

"Then there's a strong boot-lick sentiment in the class," returned the other cadet. "But I think Mr. Prescott is going to head a manlier lot than we were yesterday."

When Anstey entered their room at barracks Dodge refused to notice him, or to answer a pleasant greeting.

"I have been trying to forgive Dick Prescott for all of the past," Cadet Dodge told himself darkly. "I wanted to start a new life, for both of us, here at West Point. But the fellow won't let me. He is always getting in my way. Oh, what a laugh there'll be in Gridley, among the mucker part of the population, when they find that I'm not class president, but that Dick Prescott is!"

Even after he lay in bed, following taps, Bert Dodge could not sleep. He lay tossing restlessly, dark thoughts surging through his mind.

"No place on earth seems large enough for Dick Prescott and me together!" muttered Dodge in the dark. "Dick Prescott, if I haven't lost my cunning you shan't be here much longer."

But the forcing of Dick Prescott out of the West Point cadet corps was not easy to accomplish nor were ways of doing it to be come upon quickly.

First, Mr. Dodge realized that he was falling behind in mathematics, and for weeks he had to give all his energy to keeping a place in the class.

Finally January came and with it examinations. The plebe escapes written examinations if he has shown proficiency in the general review of the first half of the academic year. Dick and Greg got through without these "writs." Bert Dodge was compelled to face the written test in mathematics, but he made the grade and stayed on. He was gratified, for thirty-one of the plebes were dropped after this examination.

"I've got to stay on," Bert Dodge had ground out between his teeth. "If I'm to be dropped from West Point, it must be after I've found a way to send Dick Prescott back to Gridley ahead of me!"

Spring came, and still Bert's opportunity was lacking. He and Anstey greeted each other, but that was about all the communication the two held. Yet, one night, having noted the fact that for some time Dodge had seemed depressed, the Virginian asked:

"What's wrong, Mr. Dodge? Anything in which another fellow can lend a hand?"

"Nothing's wrong," replied Dodge shortly, and turned at once to his books. Still his gloom continued, and one evening not long after Anstey said to Dick and Greg:

"That townsman of yours is so deep in gloom that it's like living in an unlighted cave to be in the same room with him. What's wrong, do you suppose?"

"No telling," replied Dick. "Just disposition, I presume. He's no longer a townsman of ours, by the way."

"Do you note really savage looks on his face?" put in Cadet Holmes.

"Don't I, though!"

"Then Bert Dodge has a mean streak on and is plotting mischief to some one!"

"Is he underhanded and treacherous?" demanded Anstey quickly.

Prescott hesitated a moment, then said:

"Perhaps you'd better keep your eyes open. You're pretty close to him, and you don't want him to do anything to bring your record in question. Still, so far as any of us knows, he's been honorable and square here; so let's give the fellow his chance and say nothing to prejudice any one else."

"You're right, Dick. Still, I wish something would pull the fellow out of his gloom. It spreads thick through the whole room."

The truth was that because he could think of no feasible plan to drive Prescott from the Military Academy, Bert Dodge had become morose and irritable. But at last he thought he saw his chance.

It was May when Greg Holmes received a telegram that an aunt of his of whom he had always been fond had died. Another telegram from Greg's father to Superintendent Martin asked that the boy be allowed to go home for the funeral. After an inquiry as to Greg's standing in class, Colonel Martin granted the permission, handing Holmes the money his father had telegraphed for the purpose. When Bert Dodge saw Greg leave the Academy his eyes lighted up.

"Prescott will be alone in his room," he muttered in evil glee. "There'll be times when he'll be out; but I'll have to work quickly!" Then a gleam came into his eyes. "Prescott will be in Lieutenant Pierson's quarters talking over football plans tomorrow night. That's my chance!"

CHAPTER XIX

THE PROWLER IN QUARTERS

At eleven o'clock the next morning Bert Dodge stepped up to another cadet known as the "sick-marcher." Together they went to the hospital where Dodge reported to the medical officer in charge.

"What's the trouble, Mr. Dodge?" asked the surgeon, reaching for the plebe's pulse.

"Chills, sir, mumbled the cadet.

"Chills? Your pulse is a bit rapid, but not suspiciously so. Let me place this thermometer in your mouth."

After two minutes Captain Goodwin removed the thermometer and held it up.

"Normal," he observed, a bit puzzled. "Dead-beating," as it is called, or trying to get into the hospital when there is no need, is not unknown to the surgeons at the Military Academy. But when done, it is usually tried before a boy has been there a year. "How long have you felt this way?"

"For about twenty-four hours, sir."

"Perhaps I'd better mark you 'quarters' for twenty-four hours to come," said the surgeon, eyeing Dodge closely.

Dodge squirmed. This was what he did not want. Being ordered to quarters would keep him in his room.

"I've been fighting this off in my room, sir," replied Dodge haltingly. "I don't feel well, and I thought that a day or two here, resting in bed under a doctor's eye, might set me up."

"Very well, Mr. Dodge. I don't think anything serious has assailed you, but we'll keep you under observation for a day or two."

Captain Goodwin completed the record of the case, then pressed a button. A sergeant of the hospital corps entered.

"Steward, Mr. Dodge is to be put to bed. Full hospital diet and rest. Further instructions will be given to you later."

"Very good, sir."

Dodge followed the sergeant to a bathroom, there to undress and bathe. When he had finished he was handed some pajamas.

"Where is my regular clothing?" asked Dodge of the private who gave him the pajamas.

"Sergeant Eberlee locked them up in a locker, sir, until you're discharged."

Bert Dodge, in a furious temper, followed the private to the bed assigned to him. His clothing locked up! That clothing had figured largely in his plan in coming to the hospital.

"Now I have played the fool!" thought the cadet. "I'd planned to get out on the sly tonight, while in here officially. Now I can't get out except in pajamas in which I'd be spotted before I'd gone ten feet! Hang the fool regulations of this hospital!"

All day Dodge lay fuming. Lieutenant Doctor Herman visited

him twice, still unwilling to say nothing was wrong. For one thing, Bert was so angry that he could not eat, and that in itself is unusual in a healthy cadet who lives a very strenuous life. Anger also gave him a flushed face and an exceptional look about the eyes. Yet, there was nothing apparent to make a physician believe there was anything serious the matter.

Bert had the ward to himself, being the only patient in the building. It was eight o'clock when a man in the uniform of the hospital corps came in to turn the lights low.

"Benton!" exclaimed Dodge. "What brings you here?"

"Is that you, Mr. Dodge?" asked Private Benton, approaching Bert's bed. "I'm sorry to see you sick, sir."

"I'm not sick, Benton. But, again, what are you doing here?" Benton was an enlisted man who, for pay, had been accustomed to serving Dodge more or less surreptitiously.

"My enlistment ran out last week, sir. So I quit the cavalry to try a three-year term in the hospital corps."

Here was Cadet Dodge's opportunity! He bribed Benton to bring him his clothes and to promise silence.

"It would be time in a military prison for me if I told, sir; so you can be sure I'll keep still," was Benton's remark as he let the cadet out of a back door.

As he went softly in through the east sally port, Dodge noted with joy that almost nobody was around.

"I can get by without detection," he chuckled. He did get just inside the doorway of the subdivision in which Cadets Prescott and Holmes dwelt before he attracted attention. There he passed two yearlings.

"Is that you, Mr. Dodge?" rather sharply demanded one of

these yearlings.

"No, sir," Dodge replied in a strained voice and sped on upstairs.

"Queer," muttered one of the yearlings. "I was almost positive that was Mr. Dodge."

Dodge was by this time in Dick Prescott's darkened room. He stole over to the fireplace where he worked quickly.

"I've fixed your career here, Dick Prescott!" gloated the treacherous youth.

CHAPTER XX

CONCLUSION

Dick Prescott and a dozen other plebes who had football hopes had a spent a delightful evening in Lieutenant Pierson's quarters. They left rather early, nevertheless.

"Come to my room and talk things over, Anstey," urged Dick. "We've time before taps."

Dick ran ahead to turn on the light while Anstey mounted the stairs slowly. As he entered the room, Prescott could see from the light that entered from the corridor some one crouched over by the fireplace.

"Have I a visitor?" said Dick pleasantly. "Wait till I get a look at you."

To have run from the room would have been a confession of guilt. Moreover, Dodge heard the mounting steps of Anstey outside. So he stayed while Dick turned on the light.

"It's Dodge!" exclaimed Dick. "At last accounts you were in hospital. I'm glad you're better," the cadet went on coldly.

"I slipped out of hospital," whispered Dodge. "Don't give me away, Prescott. I'd like to get back without being seen by any one else."

"What's up?"

"Don't keep me," said Bert nervously.

"What were you doing in this room?" asked Dick, becoming suspicious.

"I forgot that Holmes was away and came to see him."

"When you found the room dark did you still think Greg was here?"

"Don't keep me now. You don't want to see me skinned, do you?"

"What were you doing by the fireplace?"

"Why - why -"

"Were you aware that in days past plebes who occupied this room had pried up two of the bricks from the base of the fireplace and had a hiding cubby there?"

"Of course not! What do you take me for?" Anstey had come to the doorway, but stayed there, blocking the passage. Prescott stepped to the fireplace and stooped as though to look under the loose bricks. Dodge, in a panic, got there before him and pulled out some papers.

"I was trying to play a prank on you and Holmes. As you've forestalled it, I don't think I'll let you know what it was," and Dodge struck a match and set the papers on fire, throwing them into the fireplace.

"Perhaps you don't mind letting me enjoy your int'resting joke with you, Mr. Dodge," drawled Anstey, coming into the room.

"It wouldn't interest you, Mr. Anstey. Its foundation lies in by-gone days back in Gridley," floundered Dodge.

"At any rate, your fire has destroyed the - ah - joke. Will you assure me, Mr. Dodge, that the joke was only a good-natured one?" asked Dick Prescott, eyeing Dodge sternly.

"I assure you of that on my honor as a cadet and a gentleman," said Dodge stiffly.

"Very well then. And now good-night." The plebe who had just perjured himself turned from Prescott toward Anstey. He saw that the Virginian did not believe him.

"Just a word, Mr. Dodge," put in Anstey. "As we are near the end of the barracks year I will not ask for a new roommate. But when we come back from the summer encampment I will see to it that my roommate is some one else."

Bert Dodge paled, then flushed crimson. "Am I entitled to a reason for that, Anstey?"

"Mister Anstey, if you please, now and always hereafter."

"Certainly, Mr. Anstey. May I ask your reason for desiring a new roommate?"

"I think I need not give my reason, Mr. Dodge," and Anstey turned his back.

Bert Dodge got out of the room somehow and made his way back to the hospital ward through the back door. Dick Prescott never learned what the "joke" was. But Dodge, back in the hospital bed, muttered:

"An anonymous letter to the superintendent of the K.C. would have fixed things and the papers would have been found! Queer that Dick Prescott always comes out on top."

It occasionally happens that an unworthy cadet leaves West Point without charges against him having been heard and passed on by the authorities. Each class in the United States

Military Academy is censor of the honor of its own members. Let a cadet be found out in a lie or other dishonorable act; and he is so avoided by his comrades that he is glad to leave the Academy. It was this power of his fellow cadets that made Dodge shiver as he lay sleepless in the hospital ward.

Cadet Holmes returned to duty and was greeted hilariously by his many friends. He was even envied, in disregard of the sad event that had given him his leave.

"You fellows make me tired," grumbled Greg. "My trip has convinced me that I'd sooner tote the water bucket at West Point than own a steam yacht and an automobile anywhere else."

Greg's fellow plebes gave a yell of approval, and even some of the upper class men nodded approvingly, if somewhat haughtily.

Hard work went on; for these were anxious days for the plebes. Would some of them be dropped at the end of this first year? No one felt certain of his merits, and all worked and studied to the exclusion of most other thoughts. But at last came the general review, then the information for which all waited was posted.

"I'm satisfied," sighed Dick, after reading the lists.

Greg's work, too, had been satisfactory, as had that of Anstey. Bert Dodge, also, had got creditably past the examiners. But eighteen of the plebes were dropped.

All the first-class men passed. So now came joyous days for all the cadets except the lowly plebes, whose only participation in the gay times that take place at this season is to stand on one side and watch.

But the night of the graduation hop came and went. The day following this was the graduation of the first class.

On the evening of this day Anstey dropped in to see Dick and Greg in their room.

"Hullo, old ramrod, and you, Holmesy! Are you pondering on the fact that you'll be an exalted yearling to-morrow?"

"I don't believe the yearling himself feels exalted - it's only the plebe that puts him on a high seat. The yearling probably looks with longing to the next and the next and the next," laughed Greg.

"Oh, I don't know. Not longing," put in Dick. "I should not want to stay here always, of course. One looks forward to shouldering real responsibilities. But I'm going to enjoy every year as I go along and not wish for the next and the next."

"Just the same, the 'next' comes," replied Anstey as he said good-night and left the room.

A little later a drum sounded at the inner entrance of the north sally port. The subdivision inspector was coming - had gone.

"Greg," whispered Cadet Prescott.

"Yes, old ramrod?"

"To-morrow will be yearling camp for us!"

What happened there and during the following year will be told in the next volume, entitled "DICK PRESCOTT'S SECOND YEAR AT WEST POINT, or, Finding the Glory of the Soldier's Life."

Choose from Thousands of 1stWorldLibrary Classics By

Ada Leverson
Adolphus William Ward
Aesop
Agatha Christie
Alexander Aaronsohn
Alexander Kielland
Alexandre Dumas
Alfred Gatty
Alfred Ollivant
Alice Duer Miller
Alice Turner Curtis
Alice Dunbar
Ambrose Bierce
Amelia E. Barr
Andrew Lang
Andrew McFarland Davis
Andy Adams
Anna Sewell
Annie Besant
Annie Hamilton Donnell
Annie Payson Call
Annonaymous
Anton Chekhov
Arnold Bennett
Arthur Conan Doyle
Arthur M. Winfield
Arthur Ransome
Atticus
B.H. Baden-Powell
B. M. Bower
Baroness Emmuska Orczy
Baroness Orczy
Basil King
Bayard Taylor
Ben Macomber
Bertha Muzzy Bower
Bjornstjerne Bjornson
Booth Tarkington
Boyd Cable
Bram Stoker
C. Collodi
C. E. Orr
C. M. Ingleby
Carolyn Wells
Catherine Parr Traill
Charles A. Eastman
Charles Dickens
Charles Dudley Warner
Charles Farrar Browne

Charles Ives
Charles Kingsley
Charles Klein
Charles Lathrop Pack
Charles Whibley
Charles Willing Beale
Charlotte M. Braeme
Charlotte M. Yonge
Charlotte Perkins Stetson
Clair W. Hayes
Clarence Day Jr.
Clarence E. Mulford
Clemence Housman
Confucius
Cornelis DeWitt Wilcox
Cyril Burleigh
D. H. Lawrence
Daniel Defoe
David Garnett
Don Carlos Janes
Donald Keyhoe
Dorothy Kilner
Dougan Clark
Douglas Fairbanks
E. Nesbit
E.P.Roe
E. Phillips Oppenheim
Edgar Rice Burroughs
Edith Van Dyne
Edith Wharton
Edward J. O'Biren
Edward S. Ellis
Edwin L. Arnold
Eleanor Atkins
Eliot Gregory
Elizabeth Gaskell
Elizabeth McCracken
Elizabeth Von Arnim
Ellem Key
Emerson Hough
Emily Dickinson
Enid Bagnold
Enilor Macartney Lane
Erasmus W. Jones
Ernie Howard Pie
Ethel Turner
Ethel Watts Mumford
Eugenie Foa
Eugene Wood

Evelyn Everett-green
Everard Cotes
F. H. Cheley
F. J. Cross
Federick Austin Ogg
Ferdinand Ossendowski
Francis Bacon
Francis Darwin
Frances Hodgson Burnett
Frances Parkinson Keyes
Frank Gee Patchin
Frank Harris
Frank Jewett Mather
Frank L. Packard
Frank V. Webster
Frederic Stewart Isham
Frederick Trevor Hill
Frederick Winslow Taylor
Friedrich Kerst
Friedrich Nietzsche
Fyodor Dostoyevsky
G.A. Henty
G.K. Chesterton
Gabrielle E. Jackson
Garrett P. Serviss
Gaston Leroux
George Ade
Geroge Bernard Shaw
George Durston
George Ebers
George Eliot
George MacDonald
George Meredith
George Orwell
George Tucker
George W. Cable
George Wharton James
Gertrude Atherton
Grace E. King
Grace Gallatin
Grant Allen
Guillermo A. Sherwell
Gulielma Zollinger
Gustav Flaubert
H. A. Cody
H. B. Irving
H.C. Bailey
H. G. Wells
H. H. Munro

H. Irving Hancock
H. Rider Haggard
H. W. C. Davis
Hamilton Wright Mabie
Hans Christian Andersen
Harold Avery
Harold McGrath
Harriet Beecher Stowe
Harry Houidini
Helent Hunt Jackson
Helen Nicolay
Hendrik Conscience
Hendy David Thoreau
Henri Barbusse
Henrik Ibsen
Henry Adams
Henry Ford
Henry Frost
Henry James
Henry Jones Ford
Henry Seton Merriman
Henry W Longfellow
Herbert A. Giles
Herbert N. Casson
Herman Hesse
Homer
Honore De Balzac
Horace Walpole
Horatio Alger Jr.
Howard Pyle
Howard R. Garis
Hugh Lofting
Hugh Walpole
Humphry Ward
Ian Maclaren
Inez Haynes Gillmore
Irving Bacheller
Israel Abrahams
Ivan Turgenev
J.G.Austin
J. Henri Fabre
J. M. Barrie
J. Macdonald Oxley
J. S. Fletcher
J. S. Knowles
J. Storer Clouston
Jack London
Jacob Abbott
James Allen
James Andrews
James Baldwin

James DeMille
James Joyce
James Lane Allen
James Lane Allen
James Oliver Curwood
James Oppenheim
James Otis
James R. Driscoll
Jane Austen
Jens Peter Jacobsen
Jerome K. Jerome
John Burroughs
John Cournos
John F. Kennedy
John Gay
John Glasworthy
John Habberton
John Joy Bell
John Kendrick Bangs
John Milton
John Philip Sousa
Jonas Lauritz Idemil Lie
Jonathan Swift
Joseph A. Altsheler
Joseph Carey
Joseph Conrad
Joseph E. Badger Jr
Joseph Hergesheimer
Joseph Jacobs
Julian Hawthrone
Julies Vernes
Justin Huntly McCarthy
Kakuzo Okakura
Kenneth Grahame
Kenneth McGaffey
Kate Langley Bosher
Kate Langley Bosher
Katherine Cecil Thurston
Katherine Stokes
L. A. Abbot
L. T. Meade
L. Frank Baum
Latta Griswold
Laura Lee Hope
Laurence Housman
Leo Tolstoy
Leonid Andreyev
Lewis Carroll
Lilian Bell
Lloyd Osbourne
Louis Tracy

Louisa May Alcott
Lucy Fitch Perkins
Lucy Maud Montgomery
Lydia Miller Middleton
Lyndon Orr
M. Corvus
M. H. Adams
Margaret E. Sangster
Margaret Vandercook
Margret Penrose
Maria Edgeworth
Maria Thompson Daviess
Mariano Azuela
Marion Polk Angellotti
Mark Overton
Mark Twain
Mary Austin
Mary Catherine Crowley
Mary Cole
Mary Hastings Bradley
Mary Roberts Rinehart
Mary Rowlandson
M. Wollstonecraft Shelley
Maud Lindsay
Max Beerbohm
Myra Kelly
Nathaniel Hawthrone
Nicolo Machiavelli
O. F. Walton
Oscar Wilde
Owen Johnson
P.G. Wodehouse
Paul and Mabel Thorne
Paul G. Tomlinson
Paul Severing
Percy Brebner
Peter B. Kyne
Plato
R. Derby Holmes
R. L. Stevenson
R. S. Ball
Rabindranath Tagore
Rahul Alvares
Ralph Henry Barbour
Ralph Waldo Emmerson
Rene Descartes
Rex Beach
Rex E. Beach
Richard Harding Davis
Richard Jefferies
Richard Le Gallienne

Robert Barr
Robert Frost
Robert Gordon Anderson
Robert L. Drake
Robert Lansing
Robert Lynd
Robert Michael Ballantyne
Robert W. Chambers
Rosa Nouchette Carey
Rudyard Kipling
Samuel B. Allison
Samuel Hopkins Adams
Sarah Bernhardt
Selma Lagerlof
Sherwood Anderson
Sigmund Freud
Standish O'Grady
Stanley Weyman
Stella Benson
Stephen Crane
Stewart Edward White
Stijn Streuvels
Swami Abhedananda

Swami Parmananda
T. S. Ackland
T. S. Arthur
The Princess Der Ling
Thomas A. Janvier
Thomas A Kempis
Thomas Anderton
Thomas Bailey Aldrich
Thomas Bulfinch
Thomas De Quincey
Thomas H. Huxley
Thomas Hardy
Thomas More
Thornton W. Burgess
U. S. Grant
Valentine Williams
Various Authors
Victor Appleton
Virginia Woolf
Walter Camp
Walter Scott
Washington Irving
Wilbur Lawton

Wilkie Collins
Willa Cather
Willard F. Baker
William Dean Howells
William le Queux
W. Makepeace Thackeray
William W. Walter
Winston Churchill
Yei Theodora Ozaki
Yogi Ramacharaka
Young E. Allison
Zane Grey

F

www.ingramcontent.com/pod-product-compliance
Lightning Source LLC
Chambersburg PA
CBHW051823170626
46807CB00003B/994